PRAISE FOR L(

'Dark, gritty and deeply unsettling'
BR Reviews

'Amazing- I couldn't put it down'
Jessica Louise Burtenshaw

'Disturbing and addictive'
Amy Westleigh

'A brilliant book with an enthralling narrative
that pulls you in from the first page and never
lets you go'
QueenOfMyWheels

'Gripping, unputdownable, and with a double
twist'
BR Reviews

'An authentic, compelling tour-de-force, from a
stunning new author'
Sam Hayes

SCREAM QUIETLY

Louise Mullins

Published in Great Britain in 2015 by Dockside publishing.

This paperback edition published in 2015.

Dockside publishing, Bristol, UK.

ISBN-13: 978-1511920810
ISBN-10: 1511920815

Printed and bound by CreateSpace
www.createspace.com

DEDICATION

To my sister

'Love is blind'
William Shakespeare, The Two Gentlemen of Verona

PROLOGUE

It was his eyes I noticed first: bright blue. They were sparkling like crystals; deep and thoughtful. Then his mouth. His smile, cheeky and bright. His teeth: perfectly straight, white. His skin; slightly tanned. He wore a white T-shirt and faded blue jeans. His build: tall and muscular. He smelt faintly of Lynx. It's his boots I remember most: Black leather. The sound they made as he walked up the stairs. How they took away the light from the bottom of the locked door.

He said I looked beautiful in my thin cotton dress. He called me pretty and we danced all night, in the dim-lit room. I watched him flinch as his guests came over to share a joke with him; laughing and spilling wine on the carpet. His face grew still and then he shrugged it off. Said he'd clean it up tomorrow. But I could see his eyes darken. Even though he smiled, I noticed his jaw tighten.

If I knew then what that meant I might not have agreed to be his girlfriend. If I knew what he was capable of I might not have allowed it to go this far. I should have realised sooner just what he meant when he told me he wanted me to be his. That he wanted to look after me and would never let me go. I should have told someone. I should have noticed what was happening. Then perhaps I wouldn't be here.

But you mustn't have regrets. You mustn't blame yourself. That's what they tell me. It wasn't my fault. I only wish I could believe them. After all that's happened that's the one thing I struggle to understand. After all I was aware of what I was doing. I knew the only way I could stop it would be to fight and I knew what would happen when I did. I knew what he'd do if I didn't go through with it. It was his life or mine.

JANUARY 2002

I listen out for the crunch of tyres on the gravel outside. I hear his footsteps on the path. The sound of the key being turned in the lock. The squeak of the door as it opens. His heavy footsteps on the mat. The thud of his boots on the cream carpet. I imagine the mud and dirt landing on the floor. How difficult it will be to vacuum while it's wet. I'll have to wait until it dries and do it later.

The smell of bolognese sauce wafting through the living room from the kitchen reminds me that I'll have to dish-up soon. I'll have to alternate between cleaning and sifting spaghetti onto plates whilst presenting him with my most pleasing smile.

He walks into the room just as I stand up from the sofa. He looks at me, then around the room as though surveying it for evidence.

'What have you been up to today?' He says.

'I finished work at two o'clock then came straight over to tidy up, ready for when you got

3

back.'

'What's that awful smell?' he says.

'Dinner. I'm making spaghetti bolognese.'

'I don't want it. Make something else,' he says.

I can't help the sigh which leaves my mouth as I walk into the kitchen and open up the fridge once more to see what I can make out of leeks, cheese, ham and potatoes.

'What are you doing?' he says.

'Ham and cheese baked potatoes?'

'I suppose that'll do,' he says.

When I return to the living room he's sitting back in the sofa with his feet up on the table and a newspaper in his hand. I look down to see a fine sprinkling of mud that he's left all the way from the front door and right up to where he sits, with a curled smile as he reads.

'I'm sorry if you feel bad for what happened. I just like to know where you are, that's all,' he says.

I nod and clasp my hands together, hoping he can't see them shaking.

'Wrong wasn't it?' he says.

'Yes.'

'Why do you say that?' he says.

I take a second longer than I intend to, enabling me enough time to think of the correct answer. Wondering what he'd say before I do.

'It's not you. It's not your fault. I should have told you where I was going.'

'That's right,' he says, turning the page, his face beaming.

'You won't do it again will you?' he says.

'Of course not.'

What else can I say?

I stand to walk back into the kitchen and step onto his foot by accident.

'Watch where you're going,' he says.

'Sorry.'

I hurry into the kitchen and sieve the spaghetti onto my plate before pouring the sauce over the top of it, all the while checking the oven to make sure the potatoes haven't burnt. By the time I have his plate ready and I'm about to sprinkle the grated cheese on top of the ham covered potatoes I hear him walk into the kitchen.

He stands behind me watching. Each time I move to layer another handful of grated cheese on top of his food my hands shake harder, until I'm dropping it onto the worktop, floor and my shoes.

'Put it in the bin. I'm not that hungry. I'm going down the pub for a pint,' he says, walking back towards the front door and grabbing his coat.

Once he slams the door behind him I fall into the wall and crouch down with my head in between my knee's. After a few minutes my hands will stop shaking and the thoughts whirling through my head will have slowed.

I can feel my heart-beat pulsing. My blood thumping in my head. Has anyone ever died from a racing heart? Is this what a heart attack feels like? Am I having one now? Am I going to die?

By the time my breathing has slowed enough for me to stand and walk over to the bin to throw his dinner out my appetite has gone.

I sit at the table and try to force the food into my mouth. It feels gluey and sticks to the roof of my mouth. It tastes of mashed up cardboard with a sour tomato cream. Bits of herbs stick in between

5

my teeth. I feel as though I'm going to vomit, but I have to eat. I can't go through another night of hunger.

Once I've eaten enough to feel full I scrape the last of it into the bin and wash the dishes before heading back into the living room.

It's been four hours since he left the house. I sit here waiting, every night. Hoping he won't be too drunk, praying he won't be too argumentative.

At last, at eleven o'clock I hear footsteps outside and the jangling of keys that won't quite fit the lock as he attempts to find the hole in the dark.

I stand and walk over to the front door, opening it slowly so as not to shock him and I stand on the other side, holding the door, waiting for him to pass through, before locking it up for the night and following him into the living room.

'Come 'ere, I've missed you,' he says.

I hesitate a moment longer than I intend to.

'What's the matter? Don't you want to give me a hug? Where's my welcome home?,' he says.

Has he forgotten he's already been back?

I walk over to him and stand in front of him, waiting for him to pull me towards him. I lean down to kiss him. He brings me closer with his arm wrapped across my back until my entire body is leaning against him.

He sits back in the sofa and opens his legs for me to sit on his lap. He reaches out and takes my chin in his hand, small and light in his large palm. He holds me with his other arm while he kisses me.

I can smell whiskey on his breath and Lynx on his T-shirt. He pulls away and looks deeply into my

6

eyes.

'Would you like me to put your jacket away?'

He leverages himself out of it and flings it at me without a word.

I take his silence to mean that he doesn't want to be with me any more and so I place the coat onto the hook and make my way upstairs.

'Where are you going?' he says.

'I thought I should leave you to relax while I get my clothes ready for work tomorrow.'

'I didn't say you could leave yet. Come back here,' he says.

I stall on the fifth step and smile as I turn around. Making my way back into the living room.

'Sit down,' he says.

I sit down onto the seat next to him. I wait for him to make the first move.

'I've got something for you,' he says, reaching into his pocket and bringing out a small grey velvet box.

He passes it to me, looking at me expectantly.

'Open it up then,' he says.

I struggle to open it, my hands shaking so much I can't get the hinges to snap in place.

'Give it here,' he says, taking the box from me and opening it, before passing it back.

Inside are two small diamond earings. The stones set on silver hoops. Delicate and sparkling.

'Put them on,' he says.

I thread the loop of one into my ear and manage to fasten the clasp. I struggle with the other one, my hand moving too fast or not at all.

'Can you help me?'

'Alright,' he says, squinting and fastening the

clasp before it's thread through my ear properly.

A sharp intake of breath is all it takes for him to stand.

'You ungrateful bitch. Why the tutting and sighing?' he says.

'It hurt for a second, that's all.'

'You don't know what it feels like to hurt,' he says.

'I didn't mean-'

'Don't apologise. I hate it when you do that. Come upstairs to bed,' he says. 'I'm tired.'

I follow him out of the living room and up the stairs to the end of the landing and into the bedroom.

I go to flick the light-switch.

'Keep the lights off,' he says. 'I've got a headache.'

You're drunk and you haven't eaten anything. I'd have a headache too if I lived as you do, I think.

I watch him struggle with his jeans. Pulling them down whilst trying to shake his T-shirt off his head with one hand still holding his shoe.

'Would you like me to help?'

'I can dress and undress myself you know. I'm not a fucking child,' he says, through gritted teeth.

I step back and start to undress myself. Lifting my dress up over my head and letting it fall to the floor. Unhooking my bra and climbing into the nightdress I left on the end of the bed, ready.

'Don't bother putting that on. Get in bed,' he says.

I swallow hard and feel my hands clench. My stomach tighten. My entire body tense. I ease myself down onto the bed and pray that whatever he wants is over quickly.

He climbs on top of me, naked. I can smell his damp skin and feel his warm breath on my neck as he edges closer, tracing a line down my stomach with his finger.

'You're such a beautiful woman aren't you?' he says.

'...Yes?'

'And you want me, don't you?' he says.

'...Yes.'

He presses his lips hard, against mine. My stomach cramps and I can feel the sickness begin to erupt from my stomach. No matter how much I squirm and try to hold my breath so that I can't smell him, I can't shake this feeling away. I continue to kiss him back, mimicking his movements. Allowing him to slide his tongue into my mouth, breathing down my throat. Pressing his weight against me with each thrust.

I know I should stop him. I know I should tell him I don't want to, not tonight. But something inside me hesitates. Do I want this? A primal urge takes over me and I find myself enjoying it. I want him inside me. I want to feel his chest against mine. His warm, damp skin gliding across my own. His breath on my neck. But then his movements grow more forceful. His hands holding my wrists. His thumbs digging into the skin as he leverages himself up, leaning all his weight on my arms.

I don't feel the pain shooting down my bones or the heavy thudding of my heart against his. I can barely hear the loud crash of something heavy smashing glass and the thudding footsteps as people bound up the stairs, one at a time.

He comes inside me as I close my eyes. Then he's being dragged off me, away from the bed. His hands behind his back as they read him his rights. He ignores them and looks back at me. Never leaving my gaze as they frog-march him out of the bedroom, through the landing and down the stairs.

I hear the door slamming against the wall in the wind, over and over again. I drag the bed-sheet across me and walk slowly down the stairs to find they've all gone.

I look to the door and then back up the stairs. I can't sleep here tonight with a broken door. I pick up the phone from the small table and dial.

'Hello, my locks have been damaged. Can you come and fit a new one?'

'Yes sure. What's your address?' the woman says.

'36 Briarly lane, Neepsend, Sheffield.'

'I'll get someone around in the hour,' she says.

I run upstairs and dress as quickly as I can, knowing that at any moment a stream of women, wearing gaunt expressions will come for their drugs and be just as shocked at my undress as they are with the state of the door.

I come back down in time to see the first of them hurry from the door and disappear behind the gorse bush, separating the garden from the driveway. I close the door and pull his coat from the hook, using it as a door-stop. Hoping it will keep the most of the cold out.

I return to the living room, taking the chair by the window so that I can keep watch for the locksmith.

Two hours later a van pulls up, parking

awkwardly on the pavement. A short, stocky man with a beard treads up the path and rings the bell.

While I wait for him to knock and drill, fixing the lock with hurried hands that shake almost as much as mine, I stand in the kitchen waiting for the kettle to boil, wondering what I should do.

He won't waste his one call on me. He'll ring his solicitor. I'll have to wait for him to get bail, if he does, and speak to him then.

I lift the lid of the bread-bin and pull out eight twenty pound notes, handing them to the man. Watching him shake his head as he leaves.

Two women knock on the door a few minutes later and I spend the next hour opening and closing the door, passing small see-through bags of white powder to them. Taking the cash they hand over from their bra's with thin bony hands before leaving the notes in a pile inside the bread-bin and checking the windows and doors are locked and secure before making my way upstairs to bed.

I've got to be up in six hours for work. I know I won't sleep unless I take something.

He said the pills the doctor gave me wouldn't work forever. He said I could sprinkle some of the brown powder from the larger bag at the back of the bread-bin into my roll-ups to help me relax. He was right of course. It did relax me. I was able to sleep better than I had in months. Only I'd found myself having to use more every night just to get the same effect.

I'd used it in the morning a couple of times this week. It had stopped my hands from shaking and my teeth and bones from aching. Though I didn't tell him in case it upset him. I know I won't be using it forever. Just as long as I need too. Just until the nightmares stop and I'm able to wake up without thrashing around in the bed.

I look down at the bruises from the last time, almost faded now. They had been deep purple and red, covering the back of my shoulders and thighs.

Rowan had to wake me up. He said he couldn't rouse me. That I'd been moaning and writhing around in the bed and had woken him up. He couldn't wake me from the dream so he'd had to pinch me.

I'd awoken to a pain on my throat. It felt as though I'd been burnt. He was sat on top of me with a satisfied look in his eyes.

'You were having a nightmare. I couldn't wake you up. I'm sorry. I had to pinch you,' he said.

'It's OK. I'm OK now.'

That was the first time. Almost six months ago now. Now I smoke heroin in a roll-up and drift off to sleep quite quickly most nights. I still wake-up sometimes with a vague sense of Rowan trying to rouse me though it happens less frequently now.

I'm glad he's here when I find myself trapped in a terrifying dream inside my own head. I don't know what will happen if I have one tonight, now that he's gone.

I layer a thick amount of the powder into my roll-up, twice the amount I usually use and smoke it down to the butt. I know I'll feel drowsy and disorientated in the morning, but I don't care.

I've barely enough time to put it into the ashtray before the warm glow of serene sleep comes to take me away. I feel as though I'm drifting, through places, time and space. I feel safe.

The thought of sleeping alone in this house tonight doesn't bother me any more.

I wake up feeling nauseous. My stomach groans and my teeth are chattering by the time I sit myself up in bed and rub my eyes. I lift myself up but my body shudders from the sudden cold that permeates the house. The duvet had been keeping me warm and now, without it, I feel exposed, vulnerable.

I walk into the bathroom and before I've finished layering toothpaste on the brush I gag. My reflexes have taken over control of my body and I feel spasms of sickness erupt from the pit of my stomach as I retch and heave into the toilet bowl.

I pick up the phone from the bedside cabinet and dial the number, as I often have to, though it doesn't get any easier.

'It's Marieke. I'm sorry I won't be able to come into work today. I've got a stomach bug.'

'Ok hun,' says, Ellie, my manager. 'Just rest up and we'll see you in a few days.'

'Thanks. I'll let you know when I'm coming in.'

I put the phone down and return to the bed, pulling the covers up to my neck so that I'm cocooned beneath the warm duvet. I close my eyes and pray that my bones will stop hurting and my limbs will cease shaking soon or I'll have to roll another cigarette laced with that stuff. It's too seductive and I know that if I do I won't leave the house all day and I have to call his solicitor and find out what's going on and get some shopping in for when he comes home.

JANUARY 2015

A man approaches me as I open the car door. The car park is clear except for us. In the dark I fumble with the bags, throwing them onto the passenger seat. I hear the eggs crack and break. 'Hurry,' I say to my daughter.

Alice bounds into the car and jumps onto the seat. Causing the car to dip and bounce as she lands in position.

'Hurry will you.'

She pulls it taught, then inserts the seat-belt. I hear it snap in place. The man's only a few steps away. He's followed us from the shop. Though I can't see his face I know he's watching us. As he walks right up to where I left the trolly, only a few feet away, I hear his low panting breath. He inches forwards and then stops.

'Frustrated mum?' he says.

I turn around. I still can't see his face. It's hidden beneath a hood. He steps forward and it's then that I can just make out a chiselled jaw in the glaze which specks the side of his face from the supermarket sign.

'Frustrated mum?' he says again.

I don't know what to say. He's either a weirdo or lonely.

'No. Just tired.'

'Go home. Have some hot chocolate,' he says.

'Yeh. I might just do that,' I say as I clamber onto the seat and slam the door quickly.

He's still there. Watching. I can feel his gaze on my shoulder. My skin crawls. The key won't fit the ignition, my hand is trembling too much to find the small indent. Finally it slots into place. I turn it quickly and the engine roars into life. I reverse without looking in the side mirror. Just missing a sale sign as I accelerate and speed off.

As I leave the car park I look into the mirror and see that he's still there. Standing with the light of the sign and the luminescent moon on his face. The back lights of the car at his feet. He's tall and stocky. Frighteningly muscled. Although he's all lit up I can still only make out the lower half of his face. A square jaw. His clothes are dark. Black or deep navy blue. A sense of foreboding causes my heart to quicken and sets me on edge as I round the corner and turn off onto the main road.

Why would a man approach a lone woman in the dark? Did he want me alone? Had my daughter not been there would he have attacked me?

As I reach the mini roundabout and follow the road to the traffic lights I catch a glimpse of the empty car park in my right mirror. I can see that he's gone. But I know he's still watching. I can feel

15

his eyes on my head. My arms tingle.

As I turn the corner my limbs grow numb. I almost push my foot down harder on the accelerator as I catch a face in the rear-view mirror. I gasp and blink. Slow down and speed up again. It's Alice.

Her face appears contorted. It's her but it's not. She's there but she's not. I feel the tingling subside but can't regain the use of my foot on the peddle properly. It's as though it's made of sponge. My foot has become weak. My hands are no longer able to control the steering wheel. It's as though some other force has come to take over the actions of driving. I'm merely here. Sitting beside her, the one who is really driving.

Of course I don't tell this to the police. They'd think I was mad. Instead I tell them how the brake felt, loose and springy. How my foot pushed hard down to the floor, yet I could feel nothing grip or tighten.

The man with the small head and the young face keeps asking me the same questions, again and again. I repeat my story. Telling them how the car eventually juddered to a halt on the verge of the grass. How the branches of the tree folded over the windscreen as though lifting out to grab at the car. The tree stopped us. We are alive. I owe my life to that tree.

He insists on a breath test. Mandatory procedure. I agree. Draw in a deep breath, then let it out in a long slow push.

'All clear,' he said.

'Of course. I don't drink.'

The car must be written off. I can smell the oil,

bursting from the pipes and flooding the grass beneath it. It's too dark to see so the officer with the small head flicks his torch on and flashes it beneath the car to show me. He calls for a recovery truck and suggests we sort it all out in the morning. It's almost past nine o'clock. We left hours ago. Where has the time gone?

The older officer with the grey hair notes down the damages and makes a list of our names, address, telephone number and date of birth.

'Just running a PNC check now, he says to his colleague.

He returns from his telephone call wearing a smile and nods to me.

'All clear, PC Jennings,' he says.

He ruffles Alices hair with his hand.

'Got a little lad about your age,' he says.

Alice hides behind my leg and smiles to him, then stands behind me looking up as I try not to show how shocked I am.

'Would you like a lift?' he says.

I nod.

'Take us home.'

'The address you gave us?' he says.

I nod again.

Alice is still shaking. I can't tell if it's from the cold night air or the horror of my screams as the car slid off the road and the only thing visible in the dark from the back of the car was the tree through the windscreen as the car smacked into it. I look down at my jeans. They're caked in mud. I think of the juddering snake the car made through the thick cut green.

I blink but it's no use. It's as though my mind

has slipped back to the seconds before the crash. I see Alice's eyes bright, wide and searching. A look of fear and confusion etched onto her face as she realises that I can't make it alright. Her mum can't stop the screeching tyres, the sound of crushed metal or the smell of oil. The hiss of petrol spout from the filters and spray the side of the car.

The window was open. Perhaps if the window had been closed the sounds and smells would have been muffled, less vivid. I can smell the damp night mist mixed with street smog and petrol. I glance back at the police car parked on the side of the road, its lights flashing and blinking in the darkness. A warning to others that an accident has happened.

I can imagine the questions and hurried guesses that passers-by will concoct as they drive past. Curious looks and thoughts as to what could have possibly caused this woman to drive off the road on a clear night, straight into a tree.

The image of that tree will be molded into my mind forever, like a reminder of the sanctity of life or a warning not to allow my thoughts to over-ride my actions in future, especially while driving.

The tree's branches curled and crusted with age. Bare except for two leaves, which as the car hits it float in the breeze. Drifting, like the sails of a ship on a late summer evening, coiled and adrift.

Much like myself, I think as I step out of the car, barely remembering getting into the police car and being driven, with Alice at my side, home. Standing at the door as I breathe in and out, in and out, in an effort to stop the rising panic forming at my throat I wonder what I'll tell him. How I'll find the words to explain what happened.

How I managed to drive a car off the road and into a tree when it was barely a year old. It had nothing wrong with it.

He comes to the door, met with the fearful glazed expression on Alice's face and my tear-stricken voice. PC Jennings stands behind us, greets Koen and tips his cap in a bid of farewell as he walks back to the car.

I watch as he closes the door and the older officer sits a moment, one hand on the steering wheel and the other on his radio.

'What the hell has happened? What were the police doing here?' he says.

'We had an accident. The brakes failed. We hit a tree and-'

'Thankfully you're both alright. As long as you and Alice are okay that's all that matters,' he says.

'The car's a write-off.'

'It doesn't matter,' he says.

I allow him to pull me close. To hold me tighter than he ever has before. I feel myself melt into him. I stay in his embrace until I feel his breath, warm on my neck, causing a chill to flood through me. I'm reminded of the man in the car-park. His piercing blue eyes. But I never saw his face, how could I possibly know what colour eyes he had?

I feel my body tighten, recoil. His chest is hard. My breath thick and I find I can't swallow. He only brings me closer to him, taking my hands. I want to pull them away, to retract and stop him from bringing them up to his waist but I can't. Not in front of the police. Not in front of our daughter.

I must act normal. Hide my face so that they can't see the tears which threaten to fall, my lip begin to quiver and my hands tremble in his.

Alice steps through the door and into the house walking right past me without a second glance, as though I'm nothing, invisible.

As Koen gently pulls on my hand and leads me in through the door I see the officer clip his radio back onto the front of his pocket and drive away.

Back inside Alice comes to Koen for a cuddle. She no longer looks at me as her protector. I see it in her eyes.

A daughters love for her father is sacred. A closeness that no mother can ever reach. Just as a father can't reach the love a mother and son share. A pact, offered to them, all of them through evolution. Something deep and rooted. Something prepared and unchangeable.

Is that why I feel that hollow sensation where my heart sits now as I think back on the times I shared with my father?

With my mother it was spent. As though it had already happened and I'd just missed it. She acted as though it was there. In the background, the past, but it would not be again. It was my fathers turn to be there. Just as it was now with Alice. Koen would be there for her. To hold and protect. To read, to listen, to joke and fool around. I was to remain, a constant, separated by this invisible wall. Tread the floors. Sweep and clean. Cook and deliver. Prepare and wash. Tidy and replace. Work and home. She would come to me when she wanted to. She always did.

I must not approach, coax or request. She would want me when she was ready, when her fathers advice and support were not enough. I guessed I would be waiting a long time. She was young. She didn't need me yet, not until then. Not until that time between childhood and adulthood, the part that makes a girl a woman. The space between believing and not wanting to; when most teenagers forget what it is to be a child. When they want to run through the garden at first light, yet are afraid of what their friends will say if they saw or found out some other way. The gap betwixt not knowing how and knowing too well, the meaning of life. The time of boys and sleep-overs, of first love and the pain of its loss. The loss of a first love feeling as though somebody has taken a pin and pierced your very soul.

If only I remembered those moments. If only I could reach out and grab at those parts of me. Those childish memories of pen tattooed names on the back of my hand, with hearts and arrows, of the flutters of butterfly's sinking deep into the pit of my being. Those moments of first boyfriends, when I'd cry if we'd gone a day without seeing each other, missing him as though he'd died. Those shared times of holding hands and walking away from our group, huddled beneath a tree at the edge of the playing fields. The ground damp and soggy beneath our feet. Black pumps on wet grass. A sloppy and hurried kiss, followed by grabbing hands and a dancing tongue. Not knowing if we were doing it right but continuing to find out. Liking it even though I'd had nothing to compare it too. But I had no memories of those days, nothing to grab onto and shake into life. It was a fuzz of darkness with only the slightest hint of light where there should be none.

A muffled voice comes to me now. Breaking my wandering thoughts. I must stop this. I can't retain this habit if I'm to sit with a client. I must focus and stop losing my concentration like this. A therapist must always be attentive to her clients needs.

I shake my head and my sight clears.

'What do you want to eat? I'll go to the take-away. You need to eat, you've had a shock. Both of you,' he says.

He scoops down and fluffs Alice's hair as I pass them and make my way into the kitchen. He plants a kiss on her forehead before she runs up the stairs to get ready for bed. He turns to me and pulls me aside.

I feel the cool steel of the sink on my palm as I flatten it against the metal. I want to feel. I need to feel something. My limbs are no longer attached to me. They extend from my body. Protruding outwards and down but they're not a part of me any more.

He draws his hand up to my face. Strokes my cheek. His hot clammy breath on my neck. The cool metal on my palm. His damp hand pressing lightly on my jaw. One finger drops to my throat. The washing machine convulses and the kitchen boards slacken and drill. The sound, a hiss to my ear. A low murmur beneath the waves of the turning and juddering machine. His groin pressed against my hip. The emptiness in the pit of my stomach gives rise to a low ache. Much like a menstrual cramp or the light throb of an orgasm.

The heat between my legs grows until I can't stand it any more. I turn and retch. Heaving into the sink. He brushes the back of my head, my hair between his fingers. The washer spits into life once more. The loud humming reverberates around me, almost as though it's talking. Saying something that only I can hear. I catch it.

'Scream quietly.'

I had lifted my head high enough to make out the words above the thrumming of the machine. Whirling and spinning, my head and the washer in sequence. I turn back to the sink and retch once more.

Later as I lay beneath the quilt watching the stars appear in the dimly lit sky I wonder what would have happened if there were more cars on the road today. If it was daylight instead of night. If a pedestrian were walking along the embankment. Would I have killed someone tonight? Would my lack of skill to stop a car from rolling and thundering into the back of something or someone have caused a much nastier accident? I shake my head and try to rid the thoughts. But as I close my eyes I can't stop the images from flooding past my eyelids.

A dark figure. Closing in on me. Is this a representation of the tree? The large dark object moving closer towards us as the car slows. The engine struggling to maintain the speed in neutral. But no, the figure is lit up. The headlights throw a bright glow onto him. His hands go up to his face, blocking out the white rays. The back lights flashing a stream of light onto his dark clothes. But they're not dark, not any more. Now he wears denim blue jeans and a white T-shirt. It clings to his muscles and shows each pit and dip of his chest. A tattoo on his arm. I can't make out what it is. His hair is cut short, blonde. His eyes are a piercing blue. They glint and widen at the sight of me. His smile...

It's when I see his smile. A cheeky grin as though he holds a secret. A smile of both knowing and charm. I'm unsure of his intentions but he seems to be waiting for something, or someone. He steps forwards and I want to turn and run. There's something about him that reminds me of that man in the car park this evening. Something unsettling, almost primal.

I shake my head once more, blink a few times and turn my head on the pillow to face my husband. I watch his chest rise and fall. The rug of hair on his chest moving in the breeze of his breath. His body is warm, so warm that he heats the bed. His frame is large, built heavy, and he's muscular all over. The body hair coats him as though it's a part of him, yet is also some form of clothing. His eyes are a mixture of jade and amber. Gemstones which protect and heal.

He's the protector. The healer. The balm to our wounds. The calm to the thrashing water. The boat on the horizon as the waves build and threaten to consume us as they climb and flood.

Alice thinks so too. I've seen it in her eyes, ever since he came to us, became a part of our lives. He has cast out a line, a thread to pull us in and bring us closer. It's him who tightens the net that we're building between us. It's he who holds us together with string.

Is there such a thing as a new chapter? Another beginning after so many others? Or is it a continuum? A winding road with small paths which lead off, returning you always to the road, to continue your life journey in drive. Is there no reverse? I know I control the gears, I know I set the pace but we're not meant to know the direction it's taking us. We're not given a map, only a gearstick and accelerator. But sometimes you need to put your foot down on the brake, sometimes slowly, sometimes hard and fast. Sometimes you do so unintentionally, slowing things down without realising it. Other times you do so deliberately in order to prevent something from happening or to try to control when it does happen. Either way we're all, in most aspects in control of our destiny. If we are then it must have been my fault.

It was my fault, that's why I didn't tell the police that my foot slipped from the brake pedal. I'd never be allowed to drive again if they knew. If they knew how my legs had grown weak, my foot numb. If they knew that I'd become blinded by the flashes of the streetlights through the trees at the side of the road. Fearful when I'd seen my daughters face through the rear-view mirror, hollow and unrecognisable, sitting on the back seat. That I'd momentarily forgotten how to control my limbs as I'd heard the sounds of the leaves grazing the side of the car as I pressed, lighter and lighter on the brake. The wheel held locked into one position in front of me as I steered off, away from the lines on the road and onto the pavement, into the field, hitting the tree.

I couldn't tell them how everything had seemed to whisper. To taunt me in muffled words, something sinister, something I'd heard before but couldn't catch the meaning of. The memory, unclear, out of reach. I imagine such memories as being cloaked in darkness, crouched down, hidden from view, silent, in the deepest corner, a recess in the back of my mind somewhere. Somewhere I'd not been before. I try to reach out and grab at it while it's still there. It grows louder and eventually I hear it. Amongst the brush of trees, the leaves dancing in the wind, a wind which picked up as we nestled ourselves down beneath the cool bed-covers.

My eyes adjust to the darkness as I open them once more and catch the face of the person laying next to me. His face shadowed and hidden, familiar yet different. His scent musky and tinged with a splatter of aftershave, oceanic and light, watery and dappled with radiance.

I nestle my head in between the crescent shape of his raised arm and shoulder. My nose pressed against his chest, breathing him in. Feeling his warm skin on mine. He shudders from the touch of my cool skin and lifts his arm before turning over. I press my body against his and try not to think of those words. 'Scream quietly.' Where had I heard that before?

I lean into him, my head resting against his shoulder. This is a rare opportunity for me to enjoy the warmth of his body and the time we share. I try to steal a glance at every object and feeling within and outside of me to remind me later. Hoping that when we have to say goodbye the memory of us together on this day will remain.

For the first time in so long I just want time to stand still. I want this moment to not end, for us to walk forever, hand in hand. Just as it should be, just as any normal couple would.

He squeezes my hand and begins to walk back towards the shops which sit opposite the bridge. I have no choice but to follow him. His fingers pressed tightly against my own, so that if I slow or try to head in another direction he gives my hand another squeeze, to remind me that I can't go anywhere. Not without him.

He stops at the edge of the bridge and draws a breath of the thick cold air. I can hear the guitar music, floating in the breeze, behind us. The busker continues to strum a delicate note, carried off in the wind as I watch Rowan pulls a cigarette from his pocket and flick the lighter.

I notice how calm he seems. Not as agitated as he was this morning. Today he appears collected, together. I smile. A genuine smile as he looks down at me, his piercing blue eyes penetrating my thoughts.

'You seem happy,' he says.

'I'm just glad that you're happy.'

I hope today will be different. I hope that today he is at peace within himself. He seems to be, though that's probably to do with his solicitor and not anything I've done or said to reassure him that I'll be able to cope when he goes away.

He's been looking at something behind me for the last ten minutes and I'm in half a mind to look back and see what or who it is when he turns back to the bridge, gazing at it with a thoughtful look in his eyes. What does he think of when he does that?

The music behind us grows temporarily louder as a song I once heard, but can't name is played as a rock ballad. Though I'm sure it's meant to be a folk song. I hadn't noticed my eyes wander from him as the beat grows steadily louder and a rough smokey voice rises up from the guitar player.

He turns to me then. I feel his eyes on the side of my head. I flick my hair back from my face to meet his gaze; take my eyes from the busker to him. He sees where my eyes have been and traces the distance back from my face to the man sitting on the floor with a hat in front of him to collect the coins that the passers-by drop into it.

'Like the music?' he says.

'It's alright.'

'It would sound better from an electric guitar, he says.

'Yes, I suppose.'

'Suppose what?' he says.

'I thought all rock music was made using electric guitars.'

He smiles. He seems pleased with my reply so I continue.

'Let's go out tonight. To a nightclub. It'll be fun. We could have a drink at home first.'

He considers this a moment.

'Yeh okay,' he says, squeezing my hand and walking me across the bridge and onto the other side of the dock.

We pass the little cafe and the old warehouse. The unused tracks of a tram beneath our feet and the disused steelworks factory to our left. Then he walks us down towards the houses and along the narrow streets home. The smell of fresh fish wafting out from air conditioning ducts at the shop fronts.

I wonder when he will ask me to move in with him. We spoke about it before he was arrested. We talked endlessly about our future together. Where we would live, what we would do, when we would marry and how many children we'd have. When would he decide it was time to make that next step?

I know I'm young but that shouldn't stop us from living our lives together or doing the things we promised we would.

He squeezes my hand as we turn the corner and cross the road opposite the post office and along down the lane where the garages are, half-rusted with piles of rubble and a few large bins left empty on their sides scattering the ground to our left.

'Are you happy now you got some air?' he says.

I nod and smile. That seems to be enough for him.

I felt ill this morning. Drained and dizzy. It was when he snuck up behind me to grab a cuddle that I froze and dropped the coffee all over the floor, burning my leg in the process that caused it. I felt sick and couldn't catch my breath. That's when I knew there was something wrong. It was the third time it had happened this week. He offered to make me an appointment with my GP and decided the walk would do me good.

We reach the end of the lane and he lets go of my hand as we turn the corner. I see him from behind. His blonde hair, cut short. The sides shaved. A single stud in one ear. The muscles of his shoulders visible through the thin coat he wears over a bright white T-shirt. His lengthy legs fit snug against the fabric of his jeans. He's gorgeous. Anyone would look at him and then at me and wonder why an older man would want a young woman like me. He's too good for me. My friends would be jealous if they met him. It's a shame he doesn't have time to get to know them.

He says it's better that I don't introduce them yet. He says there's too much going on with the investigation and work. He says we should wait until we're more settled, are more committed, before we start to invite them over for dinner.

His family visit though and his friends. Though they don't mind so much about the age gap. He says my friends might find it difficult and that we should wait until I'm older and they've started dating themselves before we start going out together with them.

When we go out this weekend we'll see some of his friends, most of them women, so I won't feel awkward.

He brings his hand out behind him for me to take and we step over the wall that separates next door's back garden from ours and come through the back door, into the house.

I follow him into the kitchen and pull my shoes

off, letting them land on the mat.

'I'll make sure there's a table for us at Blue's,' he says, dialling the number for the restaurant.

This might be the last meal we share out for a while.

'Why don't you go upstairs and change into something,' he says.

I take two of the new tablets the doctor prescribed me this morning before running up the stairs. When I get there I choose the black silk knee-length dress with the black lace, threaded bolero over the top.

I look into the mirror and contemplate which make-up I should use when I hear him thudding up the stairs.

'I forgot to give you this,' he says, handing me a bottle of champagne.

'Have a glass now,' he says, bringing two small glass's out from behind him.

'What else have you got behind your back?'

'Just this,' he says, dropping a silver necklace into my hand.

'To match your earings,' he says, leaving me with a kiss to my cheek and a naughty slap to my arse.

I think I'm in love.

He has a lot of responsibilities at work and at home, with the other things he does to bring in enough money to afford the lifestyle he wants. He works hard and he deserves a social life. We should be having fun, not worrying about the law and this stupid court case. We'll have a good night and enjoy ourselves. We can deal with the serious stuff tomorrow.

When we get to the club and stand hand in hand beside the rope separating us from the non VIP's as we wait for our entrance to be cleared I wonder how much he will drink tonight or if he will pull out a small see-through bag and dance the night away.

He nods to Dan, who stands at the door telling some drunk teenage girls to leave the door clear as they're too young to enter and pushes past a couple who look far too old to still be clubbing, holding my hand and walking me in through the double doors. Shutting out the cold night air as I feel the warm, musty heat from the dance-floor climb my bare legs.

As we walk past a group of twenty-odd year olds I can see it in their eyes. 'She's too young for you mate,' they say. One of the women leans forward to whisper something in an others ear and they continue to watch us as we turn towards the bar and seat ourselves on a stool. I glance back and catch the woman staring again, in my direction. I smile and as Rowan pass's me my drink he sees the woman glaring at me from the other side of the dance-floor.

'Don't worry about them,' he says. 'They only wish they were you.'

It took my a while to get what he was saying, but by the time I did I'd drank my third vodka and coke and didn't care.

'Are you happy?' he says, seeing my gaze falter as I notice him stuff some twenty pound notes into the pocket of his trousers and a small see-through bag fall onto the floor.

Before I answer a woman comes over and picks

the bag up from the floor and walks over to the bar.

'Well?' he says.

'Yes, of course.'

He smiles. 'Good,' he says. 'You're my girl, you know. If anyone ever touches you I'll kill them.'

I have no doubt in my mind that he would kill, but what makes him think anyone would hurt me?

One of the bar-men has his eye on our table. He's watching Rowan as though he's expecting him, at any minute, to come storming over there.

'I treat you right, don't I?' he says.

'Of course.'

'Then why do you keep looking elsewhere?' he says.

'I'm not. I was just wondering why that man over there keeps staring at you.'

'Oh him. Just ignore it. He's jealous,' he says.

'Why?'

'I've got a gorgeous girl on my arm. He wishes he had one too,' he says, leaning in to kiss me, his eyes on the bar.

Just to ensure I know what he means he puts his arm across my back and squeezes my shoulder. A couple of lads walk past as he does and one of them looks down into my eyes. I try to take my eyes away from him but he walks past us slowly and then stops, patting Rowan on the back as he does.

'Lee, come and sit down,' he says.

The man takes a seat beside Rowan, opposite me and glances back at me throughout their conversation which I assume is not meant for me to overhear, by the way they draw their faces close and lower their voice.

'Lee's a good mate of mine. Do you remember him from the party?' he says.

A vague, fleeting memory shoots through my head, offering a glimmer of a face and a smile. The same look in his eyes he gives me now, waiting for my response.

'Yes. I recognise you now. Aren't you in the army?'

'Yes. Actually I'm on a six weeks leave before heading back out,' says Lee.

'Where are you based?'

'Afghanistan. Just got back from Iraq. Had to see me old ma,' he says, smiling.

His smile is infectious. I smile back and quickly let my lips fall back into a neutral place when I see that Rowan's eyes have darkened.

We've only had a few minor blips, most of which have been caused by me looking too long at other men as I walk past them or smiling. He says I smile too much. Though there isn't anything that can't be sorted out like adults, he reminds me.

That's what I am now, an adult. It just kind of happened. One day I was sat in the garden playing with my dolls and the next I was holding hands with this tall, handsome, man.

My hand fits neatly into his. Our fingers entwined. I look down to the cut on his finger. The bruised knuckles. I want to raise his hand up and kiss it better, taste his skin on my lips, take his pain away, whatever it is. I want to help, to be there for him, to support him in salving his wounds. Not just his physical wounds.

Though most of the time it shows itself in

frustration and a deep sadness which often takes over his face, I know he feels deeply. That's one of the things which first attracted me to him.

'Are you alright?'

'Yeh, why?' he says.

'You just look sad, that's all.'

'I've got a lot on my mind,' he says.

I try to guess what he's thinking. His expressions often betray his moods I know this is a misunderstanding many people have about him. Sometimes he appears aggressive in his actions but his face shows hurt. When he's distressed he looks irritated. When he's frustrated he looks scared. Like a frightened rabbit in the glare of a cars headlights before it's hit.

I read somewhere once that depression is anger turned inwards. Perhaps anger is depression being released.

'Lee, could you watch her for a minute? I've got to sort something out. I won't be long,' he says, jumping up and knocking the table so that the drink splashes about in our glass's, leaving a thin trail of sticky liquid on the dark oak wood.

Lee smiles and leans forward.

'Are you and him alright?' he says.

'Yes. He just gets a bit moody sometimes. I'm used to it.'

'Well if you ever-'

'So what did I miss?' says Rowan, returning to the table, stuffing more notes down into his pocket and taking a long swig of his drink.

'Just talking about the army,' says Lee.

'Why? Thinking of joining up?' he says.

'I signed up before I met you actually. They said

I wouldn't pass the medical.'

Rowan laughs and Lee joins in.

'Ive got to go. I've got to get the Mrs some tinned peaches,' says Lee.

He must have noticed the confused expression on our faces and continues.

'My girlfriend Amanda's pregnant. We've been trying for a couple of years and now she's craving peaches and gravy,' he says. 'Not together,' he continues as an after-thought.

Rowan is smiling again. I smile back but he looks away and takes my hand, leading me onto the dance-floor.

'I saw the way you looked at him you know. You think he's better looking than me?' he says.

'No. He's a good person. I just know.'

'Well keep your hands to yourself, alright. He's my mate and he'd tell me if he thought you were trying it on,' he says, gripping me tighter than necessary as we bounce in front of each other to the beat of the music.

'I don't look at other men in that way, and certainly not your mates.'

'I'm only joking, you stupid girl. Come here,' he says, pulling me closer towards him and leading us into a strange euphoric dance.

But something in his eyes tells me to be careful. That I should keep my eyes to the floor as we leave the club and he claps his hand against Lee's as we pass him and walk through the open double doors and back onto the street. I can't help looking back as he holds the door to the car open for me as I step inside, seeing Lee staring right at me. As soon as I see him watching he turns away and throws his cigarette onto the floor, following his friends back into the club.

What was he trying to say before Rowan came back to the table? Something like 'if I ever need something...to, what? Call him?

We spend the entire journey back through the centre of town and home in silence. The only sound apart from the constant thudding of the music escaping the speakers in the cars sound-system is my heart beating rapidly.

When we get home I follow him through the front door and into the hallway. It smells clean, sterile. I follow him into the living room. The cushions are uncreased and the cream carpet is spotless. The TV springs to life behind me and I hear the click of the remote control being put back onto the shelf above the sofa before he goes to leave the room.

'Do you want a drink?' he says.

'Please.'

I reply quicker than I intend to. I always feel nervous when we're alone, I don't know why. Perhaps I do but I shake my head to rid the picture which zooms into focus before my eyes. I don't want to think about that any more. I don't want to ruin our evening. It might be our last together for a few months.

He returns with a large glass of vodka and lemonade. I smell the liquid before I see it. I glug it down far too quickly and feel quite giddy by the time I sit myself down on the sofa next to him, though I think it's the bubbles more than the alcohol.

He fingers the fabric of my dress. I watch his

thoughts flit briefly across his eyes before he speaks. I already know what he's going to say.

'Get this off and put on one of those dresses I bought you. The peach one looks nice,' he says, as he slumps back into the chair.

I jump up and feel the warm glow of the alcohol begin to slide through me, filling me from within. It joins the other six glass's I've already drank and becomes a glowing heat which seeps from my throat to my chest, filters down into my empty stomach and spreads through my veins. The warmth seems to spill from my pores and fill the room. At least that's what it feels like. The white walls seem brighter. The air hums with life. The sounds of the television are bubbles in the air, popping and climbing with my head.

I float up the staircase and glide back down them a few minutes later with my hair tied up high on my head. My pale, thin legs jostling down the steps. When I come to the bottom and turn back to the living room I bump into him as he walks out.

'I've gotta go somewhere. I won't be long. Stay here until I get back,' he says, before kissing my cheek and turning to the front door.

I won't move. I'll stay here all night, waiting. Wondering what time he's going to come back. Wondering what mood he'll be in when he arrives.

I sit for almost an hour. In the same spot I was in when he left. I follow the cars with my eyes as they pass the large window. I trace my fingers across the CD's in the rack, wondering which one he'd choose if he was here. I eventually grow bored and decide not to wait any longer. I take one of the CD's from the rack and walk over to the stereo. It's getting dark outside now and the street lights have taken over from the sun.

I slide the CD into the stereo and a few seconds later it roars in to life. A heavy old rock band from the seventies. The one he likes. The one I pretend to. Why do I still listen to it even when he's not around?

The beat thumps through the speakers and I find my body wants to follow the music. I go to the kitchen swaying to the sounds of the electric guitar and tapping my foot to the drum-beat as I pour myself another glass of vodka. I can't remember how much cola he would use to top it up with so I guess. I lift the glass to my lips and taste it. It's stronger than he'd make it. It bites at my tongue and slides like a dagger down my throat. I wonder if it hurts like this when those fire breathers inhale the flames on those sticks, remembering the ones we saw in the centre of town last week.

It's not long before my energy begins to drop and the alcohol floods through me. I balance myself on the edge of the sofa so that I can look out of the window at the drive whilst swapping the CD's over for another one when I remember another song I like. Eventually I see his car glide up the street and pull in to the drive. I swing my legs to the music whilst simultaneously raking through the rack to find another CD, or at least pretending to, as he turns the engine off.

I don't know why I sit and wait for the image of the car, pulling up onto the gravel driveway before I begin doing things, making it appear as though

I'm busy. Surely I'd hear the car before I saw it. The engine is loud enough. But the music is also loud. I turn it down so low that I can hear the hiss of the speakers behind the band.

At least he won't get upset. He won't get irritated if the music is turned down. Number six I think it is, the dial he leaves it set on. Or is it five? I test the strength of each number, turning and twisting the dial trying to find the right volume. In the end I settle for six. What does it matter anyway? I can always tell him it slipped a number while I was polishing it.

Sometimes when I hear the roar of the engine and then the grille descend right up to the window as though he's aiming to smash straight through it, a flood of pride and awe strike me. He's handsome, has a good job, has money, drives a nice car, buys me gifts and is not afraid of anyone. He's strong and protective. He's mine.

The flare of brilliant white head-lights flash twice as the alarm sets itself. The door squeaks as he opens it and steps out. His trainers on the gravel lap the stones and cause them to fly up as his feet slam against the ground.

It's this that tells me he's in a bad mood. That he's not been able to get what he wants, been able to sell what he needs to or do whatever it is that he wants to do. The car door slams bringing me to attention. I feel the alcohol sink and dissolve inside me. I register his temper from the way he walks, the sound his footsteps make, the quickness of his movements. The car door being slammed shut only affirms this.

I prepare a smile and a few words. Though I

don't know why. It never does any good.

His key in the lock and the door opening reminds me of the sounds my father made as he came in from work. When he returned home after a long day. Happy as he is welcomed by my mother and siblings. I always stood back and watched. I was always the last to offer him a hug or an affectionate kiss. The last to widen my eyes at his jokes and run after him, following him to the garden where the dog sat barking, as she always did for an hour before he was due home. Whatever time he came in she seemed to sense, to know before we did, when he'd be back.

The front door slams causing the pictures to shake on their hooks. The frames always giving them the security of not ever being able to fall even when the strength of the wind from the open door or the hard thud of a heavy object clattering across a room in the house threaten to drop them to the floor.

He walks past me as I stand beside the TV, my legs pressed against the heat of the radiator. The room seems to dull and bears the energy of expectancy now that he's home. I wait until he's seated before I choose where to sit.

I decide on the space between him and the corner of the sofa on the right. He pulls his shoulders in close and sniffs.

He doesn't want to be close, not now. I can feel the tension in the air. I can see the slight trembling of his hand as it lays, palm down, fingers splayed on the dark leather arm-rest of the sofa.

'Are you alright?'

Why can't I keep my thoughts inside my head

instead of blurting them out? He doesn't look alright. He looks pissed off. I wish the sofa would grow and that I'd sink into it. I wish that it would consume me, swallow me up. I wish that I'd not be here, at this moment, in this time, this place. I wish that right now he wasn't giving me that awkward silence. That he wasn't giving me that look that says, 'don't speak.' It will be better if I just keep my mouth shut.

We sit beside each other, trying not to notice one an others rigidness. I see his tongue twisting and turning in his mouth, a lump appears on his cheek then disappears as he does so. Re-appearing each time another thought crosses his mind and he presses his tongue against the inside of his cheek once more. After several agonising minutes of this he stands and walks to the door.

'Grab your coat. We're going out,' he says.

'It's late. Where are we going now?'

'Just move, will you,' he says, drawing in a large breath and blowing it back out like a sigh.

I follow him like a puppy after his mother, like a child after their parent. Is this how people see us? Him the adult, me the child. Do they see me following after him, lagging behind as he races in front, as though I can't think for myself, as though I can't think of anything else to do? I don't really do I? I act after him. I speak after he does. I match my pace with his.

I still think of him as my first love. He's my best friend. People always comment on our likeness, our ability to foresee each others movements. They don't realise that I was built this way. They don't know that I was trained to notice these things, that

I have developed the skills to notice the way he walks and the tone of his voice; the quicker his movements and the quieter his voice, the more likely it is that he's angry, that I've done or said something to upset him. It never occurred to me that most of the time he's angry with himself.

Not until today did I realise that, when he stood in some dog shit and smeared it into the carpet after taking the dog for a walk. This morning he was in a foul mood, brought on by himself, by the fact that he'd not looked down, noticed where he'd been walking. Not knowing until he was back inside the house that he'd trodden in something, his eyes elsewhere.

Instead of taking it in and allowing myself to feel his annoyance I stood back and watched, saw for the first time that outside influences caused his temper to flare up just as much as me. Perhaps I wasn't always the cause of his indifference. Maybe sometimes it was an event or situation outside of myself, something I had no control over. That didn't stop him blaming me though.

I grab my coat this time, knowing we won't be back until the early hours of the morning and head for the door. He stands holding it while I step past him. He slams the front door and then grabs my hand, rushing me over to the car. He opens the door for me, waiting for me to get inside. I loosen his grip on my hand by pulling it away from him and slide onto the seat. He slams the door in my face. What have I done now?

He turns the ignition and the engine sparks into life. The roar must annoy the neighbours. Then he presses his foot down hard on the accelerator and reverses before speeding off down the road. I see the street lights zoom past on either side of the road. The trees sweep as one in a rush of mud green, lit only by the headlights of ours and other cars passing by. By the time we reach the junction and thrust down the main road the other cars are mere shapes and colours, that you'd miss if you blinked.

We stop in the centre of town. Only a few streets away from where we left just an hour ago. The traffic has died down to a bearable thrum now that it's late. He opens the car door and holds it, waiting for me to step out.

The wind blows fierce and almost knocks me off my feet. I feel chilled to the marrow of my bones and awake. Sober, my skin tingles in the cold night air.

He slams the car door hard and locks it before holding out his hand for me to take. What if I didn't? What if I wanted to walk beside him, not pulled up against him? Why is he so protective of me? What or who is he protecting me from?

'Marieke, take my hand,' he says, grabbing it from me as I try to stuff them both into the pockets of my jacket.

We reach the front of the nightclub. A smaller one than the last. The music is thumping and the bouncer is hopping from foot to foot in an attempt to keep the bitter cold from his job. He nods at Rowan, who leads me in through the double doors and down the steps into the bar.

The music above us shakes the ceiling. A light throb begins in my temple and spreads to the socket of my right eye as he lets go of my hand

and runs over to the bar. I stand there waiting for him to return before he chooses us a seat at either end of a small round table that stands beside the sofa's, at either end of the bar.

He places two drinks down onto the table and for some reason as he does so the thought of consuming any more alcohol makes me want to heave. He waits for me to take a sip before he does the same so I pick the glass up from the table, bring it to my lips and swig it fast, not allowing myself the time to taste it.

He brings his hand down beneath the table and places it on my thigh, stroking and kneading my boney leg below the fabric of my dress. He smiles, a warm, genuine smile. A smile of love and contentment. A look of warmth and affection spreads across his face, giving him the features which again don't match his mood. I know he's frustrated with something, his foot tapping the floor, his hand clenched hard against the glass holding his drink, trembling, his knuckles white.

'I won't be long,' he says, standing up and bolstering over to the bar-man who slips from the door behind the bar and up to the serving area taking orders and slamming money into the till.

I see him lean back in surprise when Rowan appears in front of him. The bar-man wears a look of shock and paints a smile on his face to divert from the fear, which I see building behind his eyes, even from here.

What kind of business is Rowan doing with this man? The man looks over Rowan's shoulder, to where I sit, slowly sipping my drink and smiles. Whether he's smiling at me or to someone stood behind me I can't tell, but I see that this smile is real, this smile doesn't attempt to hide anything beneath it. Not like the one he gives Rowan when shaking his hand.

When Rowan returns to the table a few minutes later he's in a positive mood once more. Whatever the man at the bar said to him seems to have elevated his mood. I sit back in the chair and sip the drink, feeling my shoulders relax, knowing that everything must be alright now.

As the night wears on we dance and sing to the music, our bodies clasped together like we always were, like we were meant to be, together.

I feel as if we're alone in a room full of people. I feel as though nothing else matters but us, nothing else has meaning. We're whole together, we're one and the same, by our hearts, our minds and our bodies. He's mine, I'm his. That's how it's meant to be. We stand alone, together against the world. Moving and swaying to the music, our bodies pressed together, surrounded by people, all making the same movements, in their own worlds.

Later as he swerves the corner almost knocking the road sign over with the front end of the car, the clutch grunting and groaning under the weight of his heavy press, his feet too slow to maneuver, too quick to let go, I think how easy we are together. It's like there's an unspoken arrangement which we just live by. Neither one of us having to speak, just knowing how we're meant to be with each other. The pedal aches and groans as much as I will when I awake.

Tonight I want to wake up beside him, feel his muscles, his skin damp with sweat and heat. I want to breathe in the scent of his moisture. Feel the stroke of his lips, slightly parted against mine. I want to feel his arm wrapped across my entire body in the way that he holds me as we sleep, as though if he lets go I'll be taken from him. But I know I can't, not tonight. I have to get home.

He pulls in on the corner of the road, where my neighbours tree meets the wall in mine, where we'll not be seen. He turns the car lights out as I step out onto the road. I turn the corner and round the bend as the headlights spring back on and he turns the car around, driving off into the distance.

As I near the house I notice that I've left the lights on, the curtains still drawn. I don't want to make too much noise and arouse suspicion of my drunkenness. My neighbours are nosy. It's as I step into the flat and close the door the smell of alcohol and the musty cigarette smoke which clings to my dress reminds me of how clean and fresh Rowan's house smells in comparison.

As I pass the mirror in the hallway I notice the few droplets of spilt vodka on the bottom of my dress, my jacket is damp with perspiration and hanging off one shoulder. If that doesn't give me away to any of my neighbouring curtain-twitchers, nothing will.

I struggle with the zip of my coat and once undone throw it on to the floor beneath the mirror and head towards the bedroom. I close the door behind me and throw my clothes in a heap on the floor. I jump onto the bed and lay on my back, the quilt beneath me and stare up at the ceiling, clinging to the hope that sleep will come soon. I have to be up in four hours.

Eventually I drift, into what can only be described as a light float across the boarders between sleep and wakefulness. Alternating between temporary lack of consciousness and the veil of the dead or alert and day-dreaming.

When I do awake from the cloak of sleep I'm met with a bright day, the sun streaming through the clouds and into the window, shining a narrow line of light onto the bed where I lay. I turn and lift my hands to hold them against my head.

I can't be sure but it's as though I drank more than usual last night. In fact I can barely remember a thing, except for the pulsing drumbeat and the heaving in and out of people as we tried to find a space on the stage to dance. I only drank a few of glass's of vodka. Why does my head feel so fuzzy? Not hung-over but more like I've been hit on the head with something heavy.

Once I've thrown my dressing gown over me I walk to the bathroom and step beneath the shower. The water rains down on me in droplets of tingling heat to my chilled skin. The heating has gone off and there is little else to do to keep warm other than to take a shower or to sit in the kitchen grilling toast with the oven door open.

Through the steam which hazes the glass I begin to trace the lines of an image with my eyes. The picture came to me last night as I slept. There's Rowan, and me stood on a hill, looking up at the sky and watching the birds floating on the breeze. It's almost as hot and sticky as it is beneath the shower. My tongue sticks to the roof of my mouth. We stand apart, a foot of space between us.

Rowan's eyes were narrowed and he gazed down at his feet. His gait hung like an elderly man who'd seen too much war and pain in his life and he refused to look at me. He couldn't or wouldn't meet my eyes. I held my hand on his arm. I could feel the muscles of his biceps trembling. He was holding his tears in, stopping himself from letting them fall. I didn't know what to say or do to make it alright so I continued to watch the waves bob up and down on the horizon.

What made him so sad? What pain has he seen in this life to make him veer, ever faster, to his next?

The dream reminded me of a trip to the beach we'd taken after the party. After we'd met he'd told me he wanted to take me out somewhere. He said he wanted to see what the sun did to my face. I returned with a tan and freckles. He liked it. He said it made me look pretty.

At the beach we were seen as just another young couple enjoying a day out. What was it about the dream that made it so memorable? Rowan, I'd never seen him shrink like that. He looked vulnerable, weak, frightened. He looked as though he was about to cry. I've never seen him cry. The closest he gets to crying is a screwed up look of disappointment.

It was that same look he gave me whenever I'd done or said something to upset him. I felt just as disappointed with myself as he showed he was with me.

I know when I've done or said something to make him happy. His eyes sparkle. His smile fills his entire face, and he holds me gently. As though I'm a china doll or a crystal glass vase. Fragile and delicate. As if a sudden gust of wind will cause me to fall and break. Pieces of me shattering across the ground.

That day on the beach I planned to keep him in a good mood when everyone and everything seemed set against him. I wanted to make sure that he had nothing extra to worry about other than work or his next fight. I didn't want to be the source of his disappointment. I didn't want to bear the brunt of his frustration either.

We shared a bag of chips on the headland and I bought him an ice-cream. There was something buried beneath his smile. An unsaid agreement between his eyes and mine. A silent acknowledgement that we'd be each others, always.

I shake my head to rid the image and pull back the shower curtain. The picture is gone. Slipped from my mind as so many have done before it.

FEBRUARY 2015

I take a seat and try not to appear as restless as my mind. At the order of my supervisor I've been sent to attend eight sessions of counselling. I'm reassured that it's the usual procedure for any therapist who's been involved in an accident such as a road traffic collision, which may have been fatal. Yet I still don't see how therapy, at this time, could help me in any way. Perhaps before, when I was still training, it may have been useful then but certainly not now. Not when I feel so well. So happy, glad to be alive.

I'm fine, more than fine. I've got a new car now that the insurance company has paid out. I can see the polished exterior, it's gleaming shell sparkle and glint in the rays of sunlight beaming down on where it sits on the side of the road. Though it's still winter the air is light and cool. Not thick and damp like last year. The sun glows bright from beneath the odd cloud above the roof of the building I am inside. It's interior old and fusty, cold and unappealing.

A woman with a plum coloured cardigan draped over her shoulders, wearing a lilac and clementine blouse beneath, which seems two sizes too big for her thin frame, stands three feet away from me.

'Would you like some tea or coffee?' she says.

'No thank you.'

I know the introductions are an important aspect of building rapport with a new client but I'm not interested. I want this over with quickly. Having done this myself almost two hundred times it's maddening to be on the receiving end of such intimate questioning. I stand and follow her from the large waiting area and into a small room to the right of a little walkway.

I notice the end of the walkway leads onto an unlit staircase, and I wonder whether there are any more rooms up there. Had she asked me I might have wanted to explore the confines of a separate area, further away from the street below, and may have chosen to take my session up there. But of course a client can't choose where they'll be counselled. It's the choice of a therapist where the session will take place.

As we enter the room the woman introduces herself as Kate and waits for me to choose which seat I take before closing the door and making herself comfortable on the cream leather chair opposite me.

I feel the faux baby blue leather chair stick to the under-sides of my thighs as I dig behind me to remove the cream cushion from my back. She takes it from my hands and elegantly tosses it onto the royal blue sofa behind me. It sits low and obscure along the edge of the wall behind my chair and a table, which appears to have been used to dine on for several years before being brought up here and added to the other mis-matched furniture.

The room is small but airy. Light from the little window in front of me allows enough of the sun in to give the room a sense of being larger than it actually is, whilst allowing the room to remain homely and cosy.

A bunch of iris's sit in a lemon vase on top of a beech-wood coffee table to my left. A box of polished garden stones have been half-hazardly thrown onto the shelf beneath it. I wonder if Kate is one of those new-age counsellors who uses mindfulness and Reiki alongside her therapeutic practice. I search the room for evidence of angel figurines or a bunch of heather nailed above the door but am stunned to find there isn't any. No evidence yet that she believes in fairies or shamanic tree worship.

There's no smell to this room. The only scent is my own. A plug-in air-freshener or even a spritz of room fragrance would suffice. Still it's not my consulting room. It's not my choice what to do with the room.

I find I'm clenching my hands against the bottom of the chair in order to keep them still. Hoping that by keeping my hands down by my sides they'll cease to want to move things around in the room. I have to regain control or my need to alter the order of this room will take over my thoughts. I'm not the therapist now, I'm the client. I have to respect my therapist's choice of décor and ignore the zen garden and pile of sticks in the corner of the room behind the yellow bean-bag seats.

'Marieke, how are you finding being in the passenger seat?' she says.

I can't tell if it's nerves or whether she's chosen not to read the full report from my supervisor but this insensitive comment really grates me. I'm uncomfortable as it is without having to be reminded of the crash in this way.

'It's a little strange. I will admit.'

'From my notes you've been referred to me by your supervisor with your agreement after a rather unfortunate accident. I'd like to hear about that from you. What would you like to discuss with me here today?' she says.

'To be honest I understand being a counsellor myself the importance of being well for my clients though I don't feel I need to discuss the accident. I've come here today to show I'm willing to enter therapy myself when I need too, not because I have any unresolved issues relating to the accident...'

I pause, unsure of how much more information is relevant.

'I see. So the accident, could you tell me what it was that happened?' she says.

'It was a car accident. The brakes failed. We hit a tree.'

I see her eyes twitch as she realises that the words she chose moments ago were insensitive, but she doesn't make reference to them.

'When you say we, are you referring to somebody else being in the car with you?' she says.

Unsure of what she means I question her with my eyes and continue.

'It was me and my daughter. She was rather shaken up, we both were.'

'That is a normal reaction to the shock of such an incident. So you didn't hit anything, I mean other than the tree?' she says.

'No. In fact it was the tree that saved us in the end. I had to put the car in neutral and put the handbrake on to stop it. The car slowed, but the tree stopped the car.'

'So you and your daughter were not injured? There are no concerns with the incident in that respect?' she says.

'No. In fact I don't see the fuss in all this.'

'The counselling you mean? She says.

'Yes. It was frightening of course, and an incident I wouldn't like to repeat, but I'm perfectly fine and so is my daughter. That's all that matters isn't it?'

'Is that how you think? That so long as we are alright, alive, then everything is fine and well. No fuss needed?' she asks, looking straight at me with a smile and the widest chestnut eyes I've ever seen.

'Yes. I suppose that's right.'

'Is there anything you think I could help you with now that you are here?' she asks.

I look to the wall and see a pastel painting of a beach. A spade in the sand, sticking up beside a bucket. The water far out to the shore. The sand is yellow, the sky azure. A seagull floats softly in the breeze. I blink and then shake my head to rid the images which threaten to form in my minds eye.

'I don't think there is.'

'Well if you ever want to talk you only need to call me. This is my direct number. If I cannot answer leave a message and I will call you back as soon as I can,' she says, passing me her business card.

I take it from her and smile. Her's is warm and genuine, mine's a little forced.

I pass an older gentleman as I step outside of the room and into the waiting area. I tuck the business card into the pocket of my trousers and close the door firmly behind me.

The air outside is still and calm, reminding me of the beginnings of spring; the way the air hums with anticipation of another season. There is an obvious difference in the way the sun sits behind the clouds as if waiting for the moment that it can spring out and flood the skies with its radiant beauty.

I don't have any client's booked in for the rest of the week. Or, the week after if it were down to my supervisor. Though I've kept their appointments pencilled in my diary.

I open the car door and drop the keys at my feet. I bend down to pick them up and pull at the seat-belt as I raise myself back up into the seat. I see him across the road. The jeans first, then the jacket; black, as always. He strides without a care in the world. It's a gait of purpose and joy. He smiles to himself, caught up in a cunning thought or cheeky idea. He gives the impression of importance and ease as though every day for him is another wonderful experience.

He can't see me standing here with my mouth

open, staring. He doesn't notice my eyes shifting from him to the steering wheel and back again. But I know he feels it. I know he can feel my gaze on his back. He knows people watch him. He's aware of everything that is going on around him and I'm sure he likes it. He wants to be seen. They can't see the truth then. The closer you are to somebody the less you really know them.

I can't think where this last idea came from, that to be close to somebody means being held back from the truth, unable to see what is right in front of you. It is philosophical and most probably true, but I can't think what this has got to do with a complete stranger walking up the road, as I turn the corner slowly when the lights change.

I drive steadily, concentrating, focused. When I reach the bend in the road where the house I call home sits between two others, with much less attractive gardens, I try to think back to the day of the crash. What caused me to feel fear and anger when that man spoke to me. What was it about him? What or who did he remind me of?

I have flashes of that night but nothing much more comes of it. I have glimpses of Earth in the twilight, a shadow, the man from the car park. I can see the car screeching to a halt at the foot of the trunk as though I am above it. Watching from outside, floating above the scene. What I remember most is the loss of control, the feeling of helplessness. Knowing that I am hopelessly failing to move my limbs in time to act and stop the car.

I can picture now the scarred branches of the tree enveloping the windscreen. I can see a single leaf falling from the injured tree and landing on the glass. I can hear the branches scratch and break, bending and snapping as the front of the car smashes to a halt. But I can remember nothing of alarm. I can't see any reason for my reactions that night. I can't justify my sluggish movements. I can't comprehend why my arms and legs felt as though they were sifting through treacle. I can't tell you why my body was unable to do as my brain was instructing it to.

Why did that man in the car park frighten me so much? Why did he cause my heart to race and my body to freeze? Was it his clothes? No it was dark and though he wore a hood there was nothing intimidating about his style of dress. Was it his blue eyes? I couldn't see his face, except for his square chiseled jaw. Was it his posture? The way he held himself? No, and no. He walked and stood as a normal man.

But there was something. There was something in his voice. Something unsaid, unheard. Not his voice but the way he spoke. Not what he said but what he didn't say. His internal monologue suggested something dark and mysterious.

He'd appeared to me charming and sweet. Mild mannered and jokey. Kind and controlled. Too charming, too controlled, too sweet, too kind. Almost theatrical, as though he was playing a part in a theatre production. A player of games and of people. Was he playing a game? A mind game? Was I his pawn?

He ticks all the boxes. Every single one. But it isn't my job to diagnose or to judge. I have to be objective. I have to act respectfully to all who enter my therapy room and he's not on my list, or perhaps not anybody else's list either. He's probably just an older, lonely man, shopping late for his wife. Perhaps she forgot the milk. It's not my problem. It's not my issue. I'm wasting my time thinking over this scenario. Thinking too much, over-analysing. I shake my head and the pictures disappear. One by one they fly from my eyesight and back to wherever they come from.

I step out of the car and as I lock it up the front door swings open. Alice runs towards me, her little legs shake as she slaps the concrete with the soles of her shoes.

She appears small and needy, more so today than I've ever noticed before, except of course when she was a baby. Today though I look on her and see that she's vulnerable and weak. It's as if a sudden gust of wind will sweep her off her feet, blow her over and topple her into my arms. She's the smallest in her class but deffinitely not the quietest. This is something that she reminds me of on an almost daily basis.

She tugs at my sleeve and grabs for my hand. We skip into the house together and into the living room. I slip my shoes off and allow my feet to sink into the dark beige carpet.

Koen is seated in the chair behind the door, almost invisible. If it wasn't for the rustling of the newspaper on his lap you wouldn't know that he was in here. He pokes his head out from behind the door and smiles.

'Good day?' he says.

'Yes.'

'How'd the counselling go?' he says.

'Fine. I don't need to go back. It's just a

formality, that's all.'

'Well it's done now. You'd better go and get yourself in the shower. Dress smart. We're going out,' he says.

'Where are we going?'

'Never you mind. Just hurry up or we'll be late,' he says, standing and throwing the newspaper onto the coffee table.

I skip the stairs and pass Alice's bedroom. I catch a glimpse of two dolls stood to attention in her hands and flicked from side to side as she makes them dance. Twirling and spinning them just as I used to do as a child.

I think back to my own childhood and the times I spent enjoying the fantastical world I shared with toys, who spoke and the times I used to play with my dolls house. Believing that I was able to shrink into it so that I could eat at the dining table with Barbie and her daughter.

I never left my room. Not for years. I would have eaten in there too if my parents hadn't have had insisted on the traditional family ideal of eating at the table together to talk about your day.

I spent days in the blistering sun playing with my figures in the rockery. Making boats from old cereal boxes to take down the river, which the pond became to them. The pond was just half a foot tall. I'd invent secret societies for those who inhabited the island for which I drew maps and wrote an entire book dedicated to the local language they had to use.

I'd always had a vivid imagination. That's probably why I find it difficult to ignore the images which flood my sight sometimes. Perhaps that's why

I'm unable to sit still and just be, at one, with myself. The small snippets of memories, sensations and thoughts which drive like a spear through my head when I'm alone, with only myself for company, must be continually challenged. I challenge them through work, educational courses, personal development literature and most often- reading.

This discomforted feeling began when I was young. That's when I became a committed book- worm. I read children's story books, novels, poetry and sometimes short pieces of fiction, secretly read in snippets from the corners of the page as my mother read a magazine. Most of the books I read were mysteries; a plot to find gold or save a princess and find the hidden treasure of a sea- captain from an enchanted land, far away. Where unicorns sat gaily in sun drenched fields, a rainbow in front of them. Beneath it a treasure chest filled with diamonds, jewels and gold coins.

I believed that I would be rich and popular. Strong and free. Bold and fierce. Just like that white unicorn. A horse with the ability to fly. An animal with special powers.

That was then. Before it ended. Before my childishness gave way to a grown up sense of knowing. No longer did I look at the world with a sense of wonder, but of acknowledgement. Like an actress, I knew the lines and the role. I knew my part in the play had been laid out, set in writing. My life had been marked from the very beginning. Someone had scribbled and drawn, on easle and thread, written and noted, on paper and in books. I had been given my script and now it was time to play the part.

I was a teenager, a young adult, who knew things, who was capable of doing things, I had never known before. But how? When did I find out? How did I know? Who taught me? Who had taken on the role of teacher? Who had sat me down one day and said, 'this is who you are now. This is what you can do. Watch and listen and I will show you.'

I still wasn't sure. I wasn't sure about a lot of things, but I knew afterwards what it meant to be a woman, a grown-up. I knew what was expected of me and how to behave. I knew what a woman's body was for and I knew what it did. But I couldn't tell you now, just as I couldn't then how that had come to be. I couldn't tell you at what time things changed, when or how it happened. I just knew.

It was somewhere between my eleventh and fourteenth birthday. In that time between playing in the rockery with my dolls and developing my first crush, my first love. When I'd come to realise that I liked the scent of male skin and the touch of a slobbery mouth as a boy fumbled with my zip and tried to act as though he'd done it before.

I had. I knew what I was doing. I just didn't know how to tell him, what to say, how to show him. But I knew. I'd always known. At least that's how it felt. Perhaps I'd been here before. An old soul they sometimes call them. People who just know things they couldn't possibly have been aware of before that event or situation in which they find themselves. Unable to believe they have to do it all over again.

'Why?' they ask. 'Why have I got to go through

this all again?'

Perhaps like me they've done it all so many times before that it bores them. Nothing is a new experience. Everything is old and has already been touched.

That's how I often felt during those years, as though something had already happened. Like I'd been born twice and every few years I'd jump ahead of everyone else because I'd done this part many times before and it didn't need doing again.

I didn't need to be a twelve/thirteen year old girl again. I could go from child to adult without that space in between. Those times that my peers had to sit on the fence and await the instructions to move forward into. I'd already read the manual. I'd ripped out the pages, screwed them up and thrown them onto the fire.

That time was over now, I'd live as I wanted, be who I wanted, do what I pleased. I'd snog boys and stay out late, skip school and run off for the night. Spend the night in a dark forest without a tent or under the half fallen roof of a musty old farm house, derelict and wet with rain. I'd enjoy the soil on my knees and the trickle of water splitting the ceiling and landing on my brow. A cigarette would be passed from one to the other of us as we sat in a circle, a blazing fire between us, huddled together in blankets, telling ghost stories as we sipped from a stolen can of beer, thinking our parents wouldn't notice.

I blinked as he came up behind me, forcing my memories aside. And froze as his arms rested on my shoulders.

'Let's go,' he says.

'I haven't had time to dress.'

'Go as you are,' he says.

I pull out an old sparkly top from the wardrobe and sling it over the black vest I'm already wearing. I slip my shoes off, replacing them with my three inch high boots. I follow Koen and Alice to the car. My thoughts are half here and half somewhere else.

I don't notice as we pull into a space and the engine stops, that we've arrived. I only know that the purring hum has stopped and that my hands ache from clenching them too tightly to my handbag.

I allow Koen and Alice to step out of the car first and follow them as a child would to a parent. Unsure of where to go or what to do, I wait for them to pass through the main door first, then step in and suddenly I've stepped into another world. A place of noise and smells, of cheerfulness and balloons, a birthday party. A boy bounds in front of us chasing his sister. A waitress shows us to our table, where again I wait for him to sit first, then Alice, before taking the seat nearest the window.

I glance around and notice the atmosphere is buzzing, like electricity is pulsing the air.

'What do you want babe?' he asks.

I can't think straight. By the smells emanating from the kitchens I assume this restaurant is Italian. The garlic and tomato mean nothing to my brain right now.

'What are you having?'

'Meat feast and salad,' he says.

'I'll have the same as you.'

The waitress returns a few minutes later, after taking our orders, bringing a tray of drinks to the table. Half a pint of cola for each of us.

His eyes cast over the menu. He does this a lot, orders something and then wants to see what he could have had.

'I thought you said we were going somewhere nice?'

'Isn't this good enough for you?' he says.

'No. I mean, I thought you meant somewhere special.'

'It is special. We've not much money and the food is good here. They do a good pasta here too. Can't you remember?' he asks.

I want to say 'no I don't,' but I don't want to ruin the meal. As I watch Koen and Alice share secret glances and acknowledge observations of people or another good sounding meal from the menu my mind starts to drift again.

I'm sent back to the pulse of music and the throb of voices. The echo in the nightclub, the hazy smoke filled dance-floor, and the bodies compacted. Everyone is too close together. Hips and arms swipe us as we dance. I can remember a spilt drink, the tang on my lips of a sweet and throat warming drink.

I blink and find that Alice is looking at me, smiling. But as I lean across the table to place my hand on hers she startles.

'What's the matter mum?' she says.

'Nothing love. I'm fine.'

I send her a reassuring smile but it's too quick, and she gives me that knowing glance. The same one she gave me when I crashed the car. She has a look of knowing the truth hidden behind a person's pretence. She's too old for her boots.

A couple walk into the restaurant. The man has his arm around the woman's waist. They're laughing and obviously in love. I notice his hands, clasped a little too tight to her hip. On second glance he walks at a slightly quicker pace than her. She's almost being dragged along by him, rather than walking alongside him at her own pace.

I still don't know where all these thoughts spring from but they're becoming more annoying by the day. I've no idea who the man in my dreams, my day-dreams is, but he seems to be following me. He's not here in person but in spirit, as though he's haunting me. But do I know him? I recognise his smile. Cheeky, warm, affectionate, charming, charismatic and intent. His eyes are deep and piercing. Always focused, planning, cunning and controlled. He looks as though he can see inside me, read me. He can read my thoughts.

I'm shaken once more from my imagination when Koen brakes the spell. I blink.

'You look miles away,' he says.

'Oh I haven't been far.'

I try to laugh it off, but seeing that mans eyes again has caused me to lose my appetite.

'Pizza's here,' he says.

I don't remember ordering.

Alice hugs her father tightly as though letting go will erase him. She shuffles forwards, drawing the chair up close to the table. Her little fingers scratch away at the filling on one of the slices of pizza.

'It's hot mind,' I remind her.

She nods and continues until she has a triangle

of melted cheese and tomato in her hands. When she bites and pulls away her nose is coated with a thick layer of sauce.

'You look like Rudolph's cousin.'

She doesn't understand. She doesn't need to. I know from the way she glances at me, then at her father that this is a special moment that must be savoured. There's no need for us to speak. We can sit silently, eating. Offering the occasional glance towards the person to our right or left. We're a family. This is what families do.

Families eat together, play games together. They joke around and tidy together. They share moments like this, eating a meal out together and sleep in the same house. I tell myself that this is normal. This is what we're meant to be doing. But what is normal anyway?

As soon as we return home I run upstairs to change into my pyjamas. As I'm pulling the belt from the soft cotton dressing gown across my waist, I shudder. I can feel his eyes on me, watching. Piercing my thoughts. As though he's attempting to dissemble and attach something from them into a coherent narrative. But he won't. If I am unable to do so myself how could he?

There's something about the way a man watches his wife undress and redress. Unfurl like a flower before re-attaching her clothes and changing from covered and protected to naked and back again, which unsettles me. Is that why we dress, not merely to keep warm but also to protect ourselves?

I pull back the covers and feel the cool sheets beneath me. The soft, comforting duvet, thick above me like a leaded weight, cocooning me from the outside world. I burrow myself beneath the covers as though ready for hibernation. Koen shuffles and turns sideways so that we're able to taste each other's breath as we inhale. He brings his hand up and cups my face.

A flash of a shadow and a dark room, much darker than it is here. An image which zooms into focus as he edges closer.

It is then that I remember why that man in the car park, cloaked in darkness and malice seemed so familiar. It was the shoes. Black boots. He wore the same shoes as the man in my dreams.

MARCH 2002

The first of the daffodils have appeared on the small green. The trees are filled with tiny buds of blossom, feeding off the sun, waiting to flower. The bees are starting to clamber out from beneath their hives, hidden amongst the thick grass in holes pitted in the earth. The air smells fresh and inviting. The wind speaks of new beginnings, new life. Lambs and chicks will birth and the undergrowth will rise up from beneath them, drying and reaching out for more of their life giving food, the sun and air. Then nature and wildlife will hope for rain that won't come for many months.

I feel light on my feet and my mind is clear of all thoughts as I step in tune to the sound my sandals make as my feet climb the hill, up to the side road and along past the church to the house.

I think back to the party. The night we shared our first kiss beneath the dim-lit room. The night he called me beautiful, when he held me close and

I felt safe, protected, loved.

When I get to his I find his gym bag has gone. I'll have to make a chicken salad for tonight. He'll need the protein.

I imagine him in the ring. Animal, primal. His body tense and his movements quick. Though his face is fixed. That's how I know he'll win. He always does. It's those set features and narrowed eyes, not like the other men who's eyes widen and bulge, who's faces contort with concentrated anger and occasionally break the rules, that tell me he'll win, that he'll beat them.

Rowan's a fighter, a born fighter. He's calm and at peace, quiet and still when he's in the ring. That's what makes it all the more chilling. He's in control, he's the aggressor. His opponent is the passive pawn, the player, the victim, in a game he's designed. He seems to always know what's about to happen and when. He knows he's going to win even before the fight is over. His head rises higher above his shoulders and his eyes look down on everyone else, surveying the scene, observing his minions.

He's dangerous when he's like that. Dangerous in a way that when I first met him made me think he was a bad-boy. I thought it was life-affirming. I will the one to tame him, to hold the leash and to turn this bad-boy good. I am the one who can alter his fast responses, his reflexes which more often than not result in some form of damage or destruction. I am the one who can calm him, the only one who understands him, the only one who dares to question him.

I want to be the one to say, 'look, he's changed.

He's not as he was before. He's clean now. He's a good person. I did that. It was me. He did it. He changed for me.'

Would anybody believe me now? After so much time has lapsed, and he's already shown himself to be unreachable. Unable to be tamed and calmed. Could anybody else see what I do? Hear the softly spoken words he says to me?

After-all I'm the only one he confides in. The only one he's told of his past. I am the only person in the world who knows what he's capable of. I am the only one who knows what it means when his eyes tighten, sit almost closed on the tops of his cheeks, his hand clenched in a fist by his side, his face flushed and the tiny blood vessels beneath the skin turning purple.

I wait in the living room until I hear the car roaring up the street. The grille descend right up to the window. His pace has quickened since this morning. His face is flushed, and he has a new energy. Something less than annoyed and more than calm.

He walks into the house and glances around.

'What have you been doing today?' he says.

'I went for a walk after work-'

'With who?' he says.

'Alone.'

'Why?' he says.

'I just felt like getting some air. What do you want for dinner? I thought if you've been to the gym-'

'How do you know where I've been? Are you checking up on me?' he says.

'Of course not. I just-'

'I've got to meet someone. I'll be back late. Stay here until I get back,' he says, leaving the room quicker than when he came in and running to the door.

'But you've only just got in-'

I hear the door slam, the car speed off down the road.

A few minutes later I hear the door-bell and answer it while placing my coat on the hook.

'Karen, Hi.'

'Thought I'd pop round for a cupa. I've brought Sophie, my daughter-in-law. You don't mind do you?' she says.

'No, of course not. Come in.'

'Would you like something to drink? Tea, coffee?'

'Tea please,' she says.

I hurry to the kitchen, returning to dish out cakes and tea like the hostess. I'm the lady of the manor. I feel like one now. I feel like a woman, like a wife. Will I feel like a mother too? When it's my time, when I'm able to birth his child, when we're finally allowed to marry.

'So how's things?' says Karen.

'Fine. I've just finished work. Just pottering around the house really.'

'How's Rowan?' she says.

'Good.'

She exchanges a glance with Sophie, as though they share a thought, then she looks down into her cup.

'So how are you, both?'

'Not too bad. I need to speak to Rowan. Do you know what time he'll be back from work?' she says.

'Around six.'

She swigs her tea quickly and stands to leave. I notice how thin her arms have gone since I last saw her. The bones of her fingers visible through the tanned skin.

'I should be heading back. I've got a lot of things to be getting on with. Tell him to pop round later, will you?' she says.

'Of course. Is it important?'

She hesitates a moment.

'Not really anything to worry about. I'll see you soon,' she says, walking towards the front door, Sophie following behind her.

As they leave, Karen and Sophie press themselves against me in a mutual exchange of goodbye hugs and extended stares, hopeful that I will give something away, trust them enough to divulge some secret to them about Rowan. Why is everyone so interested in our relationship? What is it that makes them gaze at us for much longer than necessary, or to stall at the door as they leave?

I close the door on his guests, though for some reason he's never here when they visit, and walk into the kitchen to make myself another cup of tea.

I open the fridge and there on the shelf behind the cakes are twelve tiny bottles in egg-box containers. I read the words on the labels again and again, many times, until they blur and melt into one another. They tell a story, a tale, another side to the reality in which I live. I don't want to believe what they say and so I close the fridge door and return to the living room without my tea. Why did I not see them before? I've been in the fridge at least three times this afternoon?.

I could ignore the bottles themselves but not the words. I couldn't ignore the writing on the labels. Those words had etched themselves into my memory for all time. How could I have not known? How could I have been so blind, unable to see what's been right in front of me all of this time?

I settle down in front of the TV planning what to say when he gets in. Wondering how to phrase my questions without seeming nosey or critical. Wondering what kind of mood he'll be in.

When the familiar sound of the engine appears over the low murmur of voices on the TV I realise I haven't made any food. I run from the chair and into the kitchen just as I hear the car door slam and his footsteps lapping the gravel, heading towards the front door.

'What's for dinner?' he says, bounding through the door, heading straight for the kitchen, where I stand slicing chicken into strips.

'Chicken salad.'

He grunts and comes to stand behind me.

'That's a sharp knife. That would do some real damage if you had an accident,' he says, leaning his face close to my neck.

I can smell whisky and sweat. He must have forgotten to use deodorant at the gym earlier.

I feel my shoulders tense and my heart begin to race.

'Did you hear what I said,' he says, lowering his voice.

'Yes. You said-'

'I know what I said. Go and sit down. I'll finish the dinner,' he says, taking the knife from my hand.

I open my mouth to speak but only a sigh comes out. Now's not the time to ask him about the bottles. I walk back into the living room and sit at the dining table with a book in my hand. A novel I started reading months ago but never got the chance to finish.

Later as we sit and eat in silence, the clock striking nine o'clock, I watch him. His lips purse and suck on the meat, the chomping and grinding of his teeth causing me to shudder. It niggles and bites at my skin.

His phone bleeps and in between washing-up and tidying the table I over-hear snippets of conversation. 'I had to make my own dinner when I got in...the money's not as good as it used to be...thinking of selling pills this weekend...they're in the fridge...Friday night.'

I can't stop the feeling of crawling on my skin. Not even as we later lay side by side, beneath the bed-covers, the heat of his breath on my neck, the scent of Lynx on his skin. The rough hands he uses to stroke a line down from beneath my arm to my hip. The words on those bottles keep forming in front of my face. I can't stop the images of him with another woman from disrupting our time together.

Every stroke, every caress, every press of his fingers on my body jolt me back to reality as waves of visual notes linger between us while we lay together, our bodies entwined, beneath the bed-covers. Did he touch other women this way? Was he with one of them tonight? Do they know about me? Do they know I exist?

I look up from staring at his chest to try to refocus my mind and meet his eyes. His smile. Does he smile at her like this? Does he run his fingers through her hair like this? Then an image flashes through my mind once more as he brings his body hard against mine.

He smiles, runs his fingers through her hair, then tugs on it. His hands crawling and clawing at her, like a kitten to a scratching pole.

Why did he hide these things from me? Why did he live this secret life? Then I thought, he returns to me each night after spending his time with another woman, another girl. He shares his body with them, but I share his mind.

I try to relax, allowing him to direct me, my hands following his, rocking against him to the pace he's set. My skin tingles. My body rigid and my movements tense. It's no good, I can't stay here and think. I can't stop these images swarming through my head. I have to get up, I have to get out of here. I can't breathe. I feel trapped. In this moment I feel as though I'm a prisoner, held captive within the arms of my own boyfriend as he presses his skin tight against mine, his arms, too strong, gripping me close, preventing me from pulling away.

I lift my head and try to push myself back into the soft mattress of the bed to free myself of his grip but he holds me too tight. His arm is draped across my body so that I'm unable to move. I can't get up. I can't escape.

'Rowan, I have to get up.'

'Stay here. I want you to stay with me,' he says.

'I will. I just have to go to the toilet.'

He lifts his arm up and I'm free. I spring from the bed a little too quickly. I run to the bathroom a little too fast. I spend much too long in there mulling things over. When I come out and return to the bedroom he's waiting for me, sat up in bed. He's listening to my thoughts. He knows what I'm going to say. He knows what words I've been rehearsing in my head. He knows I want to leave, but I hope he doesn't know why.

'Where are you going?' he says.

'Nowhere. I just needed the toilet.'

'You want to go home. That's fine. But come here first. I want to give you something,' he says.

His eyes crease. His body tightens. His fist is hidden beneath the quilt, but I know it's clenched. I know what he wants and this time I'm not going to let him have it.

I don't know what has taken me over. I'm suddenly aware of my surroundings more than I had been. Everything seems brighter, bolder. The air is still and quiet. It's the calm before the storm.

He draws his hand up, motioning for me to come towards him. I follow obediently as though he's my master and I'm his dog. He takes my hand and stands from the bed. He leads me over to the corner of the room where the full length mirror stands imposing, blocking one door of the wardrobe.

'Take your clothes off,' he says.

Has he bought me another dress, another expensive set of lingerie?

'Come on, take them off,' he says.

I'm only wearing my pyjama top and a pair of knickers. He'd not removed all of my clothes yet.

I feel embarrassed, vulnerable. I take a long time to remove my clothes, deliberately, to show him how much I really don't want to do this. Once they are off and tossed onto the chair at the end of the bed he looks at the floor and then back at me. He stares at me for a moment, my back to him. He stands behind me watching my expression in the mirror. He sees my eyes look from the floor up to the mirror and back to my feet several times before he says another word.

'Look,' he says.

I'm wondering where my present is. This gift that he suggested was special and clothing related in my mind.

I hear him sigh. A deep, slightly irritated outlet of breath. He's impatient and annoyed but I'm going to take my time. Whatever it is that he wants it can't be only to see me dress into a new outfit. It must be something else.

'Look,' he says.

I remember all the times he's told me how beautiful I am, how happy I make him feel, how blue my eyes are compared with his, how blonde my hair is to his slightly darker shade. He tells me that my smile is gentle and my body feminine. He breaks the spell with another sign. My reminiscence of the past year is being slowly erased as he repeats himself once more. I know this is the last time he will before he loses it.

'Look in the mirror,' he says, his voice breaking slightly.

I bring my gaze up to meet his eyes in the mirror. He smiles. There's something behind his smile. Something malicious and sinister sits beneath his grin, something I can't quite reason.

'Look at yourself,' he says, lowering his voice to a whisper, as though we're not alone in this room.

I look down at my feet, then follow upwards from my painted nails to my thighs and chest, up to my chin, then at last my own eyes.

He steps forward and brushes the hair back from behind my head, holding it up as he leans in, close to my neck so that I can feel the heat of his breath on my skin.

'You're fat. You need to lose some weight,' he says.

I look down from my own eyes staring back at me in shock. I look down at my hips, the skin pulled tight against the bones. I look at my chest, two small mounds of flesh just below my collar bone. Breasts almost flat and boyish. Above them my collar bone juts out, like a tree branch beneath a sheet caught in the wind. My eyes are hollow, sunken. There's dark circles beneath them. My legs are fleshy and wobbly. I move my gaze back over to my hips and see the skin covering the bones, thick masses of it. My chest droopy, breasts sagging. Oh yes, I'm fat.

He steps back so that he can see my reflection in the mirror. He meets my eyes, sees a single tear well up in one corner, my nose twitch hoping this will stop it from falling.

I can't cry. I can't show negative emotions. I can't show him that he's upset me, that he's hurt me. I won't give him a reason to believe that he's got one over on me, that he's won.

He walks away, out of the room and down the stairs. I stand there motionless. Unable to think of anything but those words. Where's he gone? It's late. We should be in bed, sleeping.

I return to bed. Deciding to wait for him to come back upstairs. I'm hungry. I feel genuine hunger for the first time in so long that I almost forget what this feeling means. It's not only a hunger for food, for nourishment but a need, a primal urge to fill myself, my empty stomach. I want to fill the hollow pit where my flabby skin coats the emptiness within. I want to eat something, anything until I feel sick. I want to fill myself to the brim by gorging on crisps and meat and cake and apples.

As I drift into sleep the hunger subsides as I dream of stuffing myself with cake, crisps and sandwiches, until at last, by morning it's a dull ache. I feel sick and my stomach rumbles. I want to eat but skip breakfast.

I must remember what he said. I must think of those words every time I feel that hunger from now on, I'm fat and I must lose weight. If I do nothing about my weight he might not want me any more. He'll stop loving me. I can't afford for him to stop loving me. Nobody else would want me, not like this.

He didn't return to bed last night. I thought it might have been because I disgust him. Perhaps he didn't want to look at me any more. But a part of me, just a small part, wondered if what he saw was right. Was I fat? Or did he just think I was?

Later, in work I give up trying to ignore the constant growling of my stomach, the nauseating crush of emptiness. I down two mugs of steaming coffee and try to stay awake and stuff my face with a sandwich, a bar of chocolate and two slices of thick creamy jam sponge cake. I feel awful for doing it and wish I hadn't as I feel it sink and set inside me. But I'm secretly glad, proud of myself for lasting an entire night and morning before eating, happy when I think of the calories I've probably lost already.

By the time I get back to his I feel sick with regret. When he looks at me, just a glance, as I pass him in the hallway, remorse over my greedy actions takes over the hunger. A tightening knot of dread for what I've done to myself and the realisation that I've failed, once more. What will become of me now that I've eaten so much food. These thoughts wash over me in waves as I offer him a smile he doesn't return and walk up the stairs.

By the time I reach the bathroom I know what I have to do. It's like a light has switched on in my brain and I've finally remembered, something previously read in a book or magazine article. I'll purge myself, rid myself of this feeling.

I lock the door behind me and stick my fingers down my throat. I retch and rid myself of the food, knowing that the nutrients will have already begun to digest so all that I'm doing is ridding the bad food from my body. The sugar and salt, the unhealthy and fattening ingredients are leaving me.

I hear him stomp up the stairs. When he reaches the top he stands on the other side of the door, listening, waiting.

'Are you in there,' he says.

'Yes. I'll be out in a minute.'

I find him waiting outside the bathroom door,

standing with a knowing look in his eye. I'm sure that my secret is already out, but he gives nothing away.

He doesn't ask me what I was doing up there earlier, why I'd spent so long in the bathroom. We sit opposite each other at the dining table, a loaded plate of meat and vegetables in front of us.

'You look ill. You need to eat. Here this will fatten you up,' he says, slamming a steaming jug of gravy down onto the table beside my plate.

Did I just hear him right? Yesterday I was fat, today I look ill and need fattening up. Is he loosing his mind, or am I?

I lift the fork and taste the food. I allow my senses to leave me and continue to force the food down my throat until the plate is empty. No sooner have I finished does he leave the table, returning a few seconds later with a steaming bowl of chocolate pudding.

'You gotta eat,' he says.

I take this as a signal to do so and quickly finish the bowl. Aware that he's not given himself a bowl of pudding and is no longer eating. Though he seems to be enjoying watching me as I cram every last spoonful into my mouth and swallow hard, enjoying the feeling of being so full, but remembering to savour the feeing of emptiness later as I repeat the process of filling, gorging and purging and ridding in a cycle to which there must be one end, one result- loosing weight.

As he stands to clear the plates away I realise how heavy and full I feel now. I wonder how many calories I've consumed.

I grab my bowl and the gravy jug and follow

him into the kitchen. He stops still as though considering something then turns, gazing at me for a few moments.

'I didn't think you'd eat all that. You really are a fat cow aren't you,' he says.

He shows no emotion in his face as he speaks. It's neither a joke nor a criticism. He's merely stating a fact, making an observation. But I see his eyes narrowing and his voice quiver as though he doesn't mean to say those words, but he's got no choice.

Is this a game? Am I playing along as he expects? Does he want me to disagree? Does he want me to stick up for myself? Does he want an argument? I'm not in the mood and so I place my bowl in the sink, along with the jug and leave the room without a word.

Upstairs I fall into a heap on the sheets. They cling to my wet face as I try to breathe, in and out, in and out. I don't know what to do. I don't know what is expected of me and so I just stay here, with the quilt on my face, hiding. Covering over the cracks in my head, the twisted knots in my brain.

He comes up the stairs and joins me later. He takes my arms and turns me over onto my back. I let him, like I always do. He wants to make it up to me and so I play along, pretending. I know so well how to do this. Pretending to be alright, painting a fake smile on my face, but it's not this he wants. Why am I making this so easy for him? He enjoys the fight, the struggle.

His voice lowers. His eyes grip mine. I can't look away, in yet I can't hold his gaze. I'm frozen. I feel my body as though it's another entity, another shell, one that I can shed and leave behind any time I want.

I must have drank a lot last night. I can't remember a thing. Only the glass on the bed-side table, half filled with the remnants of vodka and coke tell me that I drank, that I feel woozy from the alcohol and not something else.

When did we get up, go downstairs and drink, then come back to bed?

I draw my hand out and feel his side of the bed is empty.

'Rowan?'

My voice sounds muffled. My lips are numb. One side of my face sticks to the covers, wet. I lift my head and see the pillow is covered with blood. I lift my hand to my face to see, then bring it back down. Thick congealed scarlet sits on my hand. I wipe it on the bed-covers.

I twist and turn to pull the quilt away from me and stand, only to fall back down on the bed. My head is heavy and the room is thick. The air a solid mass. I try again to stand, but find my legs give way no sooner than my feet touch the carpet.

I drag myself across the room and along the hallway, holding on to cupboards, door handles and anything else I can grab without having to turn my head to look.

I make it to the bathroom and stand at the sink, both knowing I have to and not wanting to see my reflection. I raise my head and catch her in the mirror.

She doesn't look like me. Her face has been pummeled. A deep cut hidden within the folds of her hair has dyed it red. Her left eye is bruised and swollen. Her ribs hurt to touch and her legs are weak.

Realising I'm still dressed in yesterdays clothes I decide to take a shower, to rinse the suffocating dread from my skin, hoping that it will erase all thoughts of what may have happened last night from my mind. I want to feel the water cascade down my body and take away the pain and suffering of my wounded limbs. I want to wash away the grime and dirt, but I can't.

I can't take a shower. I have no idea who did this to me or why. Whoever did this to me might still be here. They might have hurt Rowan. I have to find him. I have to know that he's alright.

MARCH 2015

My first client of the day was a woman who'd been many times before. Each time she spent the majority of the session gazing out of the window at the dimly lit day ahead as though waiting for something to change, something to happen. Nothing would of course.

The silence built to almost impossible amounts. I found it difficult to develop empathy for somebody who was unable to meet my eyes. Somebody who spoke only to say, 'hello' and then sat staring, occasionally moving her mouth, lips opening and closing, parting and being brought back together again, muttering to herself. Her internal monologue taking over the reality of the situation. I often thought that she could rent a room for an hour each week and have the space to do the same thing, without the need of me at all.

I can't stand much more of this so I break the silence and speak. Knowing this usually results in nothing, but I want to try a different approach today.

'Heather, I wonder if you would find it easier to speak to me through modes other than speech.'

I walk over to the filing cabinet where I keep my notes and produce an A4 notebook and pen. Handing it to her before seating myself back in the chair, mirroring her position, legs together, arms by my sides, hands clasped as though in prayer.

She blinks and looks up, takes the pen and drums it against the notebook, playing with it like a child who's not sure what the teacher expects her to do.

'Some things are too difficult to put into words but many of my clients find it therapeutic and often liberating to share with me their thoughts in writing. Perhaps you could think now what you're feeling in this moment and write it down.'

She considers my words for a few moments before opening the notepad up and folding the page down behind the front cover. She takes the pen and writes one word.

'What do I do now?' she says.

'What would you like to do?'

She looks left as though somebody unseen has spoken to her, told her what to do, then passes the notebook back to me.

There is one word written neatly at the top of the page, 'sorry.'

'What are you sorry for?'

I pass her back the notebook. She writes two words and passes the notebook back to me.

It says 'Being stupid.'

'Why do you think that you're stupid?'

This time she takes the notebook from my lap and writes a short sentence. When she passes it to me I see that she has written 'I didn't know what he wanted until it was too late.'

'What did he want? And who is he?'

She drops her gaze from me to the floor and writes, this time with an almost childish pen-stroke. When she passes the notebook back to me I see she has written a short paragraph. At least we're getting somewhere. I feel genuinely proud of her achievement. She's written honestly and powerfully. I read the words, scrawled and crooked, larger than before, almost like a child's hand-writing.

She's written, 'I thought he was my friend, but he wanted something more. I didn't want to and now I feel ashamed.'

I'm surprised by her candid and poignant message. I want to ask her how old she was, what she means by 'not wanting to,' but I wait a moment as she seems to be slightly more fluid. Her movements are easy and her posture has altered. I'm suddenly made aware of the difference in her features. She looks young and vulnerable. She's smiling. A child-like mannerism which doesn't fit the situation. Instead I ask her how old she is.

'Twelve,' she says, then giggles.

'How old is he?'

'Who?' she says.

'The man you told me about?'

'I'm not allowed to speak about him,' she says.

'What was it that he made you do, that made you feel ashamed?'

Her face changes. From happy and smiling to a look of disgust and annoyance. Confusion and irritability briefly flit across her face, like the shadow of a cloud over a sun drenched lawn. We've made a sudden and profound break-through and I don't want to let this moment drift. I want to stay focused, to keep her in this time, this event that she is experiencing. Though I know I'm treading dangerous ground. Of all my clients who have experienced a trauma I've never seen this before. This complete dissociation. Reverting back to a former self, a child. I know how she got here but I've no way of knowing how to get her out of it.

'Heather, do you remember?'

I draw myself closer, still seated in the chair. My top half mirroring her bent over posture. She's holding her stomach, I hold mine. She begins to rock, I follow her.

'Heather, do you remember? Do you know what the man did?'

'Nobody knows. Nobody can ever know,' she says.

She stops rocking and looks me in the eyes.

'Don't you tell. Don't you say a thing to anyone or he will get us both,' she says.

Her face distorts. I don't know whether she's going to laugh or cry, shout and swear or lunge forwards and stab me with the pen, and so I sit back. I don't want her to feel as though this is a confrontation. The only confrontation I want to occur in these rooms is her against her abuser, and that must be done in role-play. The empty chair where she imagines he's sitting, opposite her. Where she'll stand, taller, more powerful and in charge. Just as she wasn't able to be before. But that must be done later, much further down the line. I've got her talking, that's the main thing. That's always the hardest part.

She drops her head in her hands and begins to weep. The weeping turns to sobbing and once she's spent she takes the tissue from my outstretched hand and dries her eyes.

She looks up and stares at me for a few moments. Her appearance changes back to that of the adult woman I know. She stands and throws the used tissue in the bin. She waits for me to offer her back the seat but refuses.

'I must get home. I've got a lot of jobs around the house that need doing,' she says.

'Would you like to take a few minutes to wind down? That was a breakthrough Heather. You may need some time to re-ground yourself in the present.'

'No. I feel fine, just a little sleepy,' she says.

'Has that happened before?'

'Has what happened before?' she says.

'Slipping through time like that. It's termed dissociation. You slip back into the past and experience an event or situation as though it's happening again.'

'I don't know. Maybe. Does it matter?' she says.

'It does if it interferes in your normal functioning. If it becomes dangerous.'

'Dangerous? I hardly think remembering can be dangerous,' she says, a look of confusion and irritation flits across her face again.

'If it happens while driving or-'

I stop suddenly aware that something doesn't feel right. Something hollow and painful sits in the lower half of my stomach as I continue.

'Do you know when it's going to happen or do you just come out of it as though you've been asleep, dreaming?'

'Sometimes it's like a fog descends over me. A fog I can't control. Other times I see things, hear things, smell things and then it all goes dark,' she says.

'I think it'll be helpful to note down those moments so that you can gain a clear picture of when it happens and what circumstances cause it to happen. Will you do that for me?'

'Yes. If it will help,' she says.

'I think it will. Bring the notes with you to your next session. We can work our way through this together now. You're not alone.'

'Thank you,' she says, before turning and walking out of the door and through to the front of the office, where my next client sits waiting.

'Mr Woods, would you like to come in now?'

He nods and stands, making his way to the open door of the consulting room.

I'm aware I'm running late, having gone over session with Heather and don't have time to break. The usual ten minute rest between clients is vital for both them and me. Offering me the time to evaluate and ground myself ready for the next story, the next narrative. But I'm not able to do this now and that extra ten minutes with Heather will stop me from being able to take a break before lunch; shortening my lunch hour and my time.

Mr woods has been attending for Cognitive Behavioural Therapy for several weeks now. He's shown great improvements. He's able to read his thoughts and feelings and link them to the events which cause his automatic response to depression. Which is most often to project his feelings onto others and behave as though in denial of his own shortcomings.

We end the session with a discussion relating to one of his most recent lapses into projection. He has begun to rebuild his relationship with his daughter but often finds it difficult to empathise with her difficulties, being a young adult, and so has now told her she will not be coming to his wedding to his second wife, her step-mother, because she refuses to dye her hair back to blonde. The blue and black it is now will not do for such an occasion as his wedding.

He's recognised his own part in the argument and is happy to divulge his annoyance as being related to when he was not allowed to dye his hair orange and green during his punk phase. He wants his daughter to realise this, and so I've suggested he speaks openly to her about his own teenage years to build some common ground. He's happy to do this.

He leaves as I leaf through my folder to take a quick glance at the notes for my next client. After waiting for twenty minutes I decide she's not going to turn up again and set down to write a letter to her. I tell her I must charge her again for this missed session and that I'd like to speak with her, even if only to close our sessions if she feels she no longer needs to attend counselling.

Before I fold the paper to place it into the envelope, ready on the desk, I notice the name written at the top of the letter. I've addressed it to

Rowan.

Annoyed with myself I decide to rewrite the letter after my afternoon clients and leave the letter inside the drawer. Locking it up tight and grabbing my handbag I move to the door. I'm about to open it up when a tall man appears at the window. I walk to the door and as I open it he smiles.

'Have you got a minute?' he asks.

'I'm closing up for lunch. Are you looking for something or somebody in particular?'

'I was hoping somebody could help me. I'm looking for a counsellor. I heard she was very good,' he says, passing me a business card.

I see my name written at the top. I'd forgotten I'd put these out. It seems like so long ago now. Two years have passed since I swamped the local shops and newspapers with my advertisements. Now most of my referrals are from word of mouth or doctors surgeries.

'I'm fully booked today but let me see if I can fit you in next week.'

He remains standing in the doorway while I grab a pen from the desk and leaf through the calendar I keep in the bottom drawer.

'How about next Monday?'

'Yes, that will be fine,' he says.

'Eleven o'clock?'

'Excellent. See you then,' he says.

Excellent. Wonderful. Fabulous. Such exaggerated words of happiness. Words of joy and brilliance. He seems warm. Polite and positive. What on earth could he want to discuss with me? I'll have to wait a week to find out. I close and lock the door behind me and head to the bakery.

Later, as my final client leaves the therapy centre and I lock the door behind her I take a seat in the room I use and ground myself with a meditative ritual of breathing in and out three times quickly, then slower and slower until I've calmed my breath and my arms feel heavy and relaxed.

I can't help my thoughts from over-riding the silence. The empty rooms, the building quiet and still. My mind races. Idea's and pieces of dialogue captured throughout the day whirl and run, jump and spin through my head until I can't think clearly; can't feel my feet. My arms grow stiff and tense, my movements become slow, worn and weary. Just as they had before the crash. Before the unsettling feeling began to creep up on me, as it often does at the strangest of times. Like when in session with a client, or today when I began to explain to Heather about the seriousness of her condition.

I realised then what I'd forgotten to do. I'd not suggested she makes an appointment with her doctor. I'd not requested that she mention it to a medical professional at all. What was I thinking? Why had my training and skills, experience and care not been used to its highest of standards today?

As a stress and trauma specialist I often work with the most damaged of souls, the ones who need the longest time to adjust and make changes. The kind of clients who spend sessions crying and screaming, or who become hostile and silent, punishing me as they see me as the all powerful wizard who knows what is wrong with them, how to help them and who chooses not to offer them the secret life code that enables them to erase all unwanted memories and thoughts from their minds as they continue acting and thinking the same way wondering why they can never move on. The same results and consequences occur, yet they continue to do everything I tell them to. Which I'd tell them was nothing. Because it's not my job to advise people on what to do. I can only suggest what changes they can make and hope that they implement at least some of my ideas. They most often come to the conclusion, through a sudden and profound realisation, much like a spiritual awakening, that they must think or act differently if they're to gain the result that they need to progress, to move on, with their lives. As if the idea came from themselves or God.

Still I sit and think back to my conversation with Heather. What was I trying to say? Don't drive, dissociation can be dangerous. If you're driving you could crash.

The thought unsettles me. That low ache re-appears in the deepest parts of me, Where my empty and hollow womb lies, thick and heavy, and uneasy. A reminder that something is not quite right. Something difficult. Something black. Something not of this world, this place or this time. Something fear evoking, something I can't quite grasp as this feeling settles itself in me and my arms begin to shake in an attempt to be rid of it.

Perhaps she was right. Perhaps my supervisor had been right all along. The crash has affected me more than I thought it had, more than I wanted to believe.

I take the letter from the drawer and re-write it,

using my clients name, instead of that name. I drop it into the post-box on the way to the car and drive home, knowing what I have to do.

I call Kate first to book in another session, then I call my supervisor to let her know that I'm taking a few days break. She hadn't looked pleased when I'd told her I was going to return to work after just four days off and one counselling session. I can imagine her smiling now that I've changed my mind.

Of course you're not supposed to show your thoughts and feelings so visibly in this line of work. You're meant to use a poker face; neutral and objective expressions as well as words. But I think that by just one more session with Kate and the rest of the week off I can show both of them that I'm willing to put in the effort to reflect on my position and role as a therapist in light of what I've recently experienced and take the time to consider what impact the crash has had on me.

It's only as I cross the roundabout and turn right at the junction that I notice something odd. Something that didn't quite fit the puzzle I was building. I'm driving and I feel fine. I don't feel nervous, anxious, agitated or in any other way negative about the act of driving. I feel calm, relaxed, serene even. If it's driving, the car or the accident that's unsettled me then surely I wouldn't be able to drive now, would I?

I continue to consider this as I turn left onto Maple Road and cross the empty factory. The high topped houses left derelict after the loss of employment. The lack of income bringing more and more people out of the cities and into the small towns and villages seeking work. The worst of it has passed but there is still hostility in the air, a complete lack of communion.

The communities are no longer built on the strength of work, income and shared activities No longer do people Spend their Saturday evenings in the local pub, sharing the school-run, taking their children on days out, trips to the sea or a walk in the park. Instead everyone sits inside their houses, trying to keep warm. Their only trip out is to the local shop, using the last of their benefits to buy a loaf of bread for the week. Hoping the milk will last until the following Monday.

I'm not that bad off. We're struggling just as anyone but at least we have enough money to cover the basics. The food, electricity, heating, water, petrol and the other household costs are covered. Most of our neighbours and probably most of the other people living this side of Sheffield do. But on the other side, beside the old factory works and steel houses, that's where the money needs to be spent.

Children much younger than Alice stand in the doorways of empty, boarded-up shops looking bored. The owner's no longer able to afford the business rates to keep them open have been forced to close them up. Those children look haunted, by poverty and stress. Their clothes are unwashed. They have dirty faces, broken shoes and have pale skin, covering thin bones. Wearing their older siblings oversized clothes.

Their parents are having to sign-up for a doorstep loan to pay for their packed lunch, to buy them a school jumper or a pencil case. They're the ones who need help. They're the families who need support, money, security and protection. Not us in our fancy houses, with a car filled to the brim with petrol. We don't need anything. We're alright. I know that's how they think. That's how everyone thinks; that those of us who work have it easy. They don't see the sacrifices we have to make. Missing out on the school play, skipping meals at work to get home sooner to help our children with their home-work. Working right up to Christmas just to afford the presents they hope they'll find under the tree. Filling stockings with pound-shop toys and cheap sweets to make it look as though we're like all the other families on the block; able to afford the latest gadgets.

We have our own issues though. I have my own problems; not always financially related. Sometimes in the deepest darkest of nights as I lay beneath the covers, in between dreaming and wakefulness I see things, hear things, smell things that I thought I'd forgotten.

Like now as I reach the front door, home. I tread the path and remember. Things I'd long ago forgotten. A past that has almost been replaced with love, safety and happiness. But even the way the trees sway in the wind or the sounds of the seasons as they come to replace the old fill the air around me I can sense a darkness. A deep rooted evil that once I knew but have suppressed. What it is or why I've chosen to avoid it I can't say. But I know it's there and that it'll never leave me.

In the distance I can see a trail of smoke, puffing and bellowing. Grey and blue, black and mud. Piling up and filtering out into the sky from the last place that stands where metal is formed and reduced. Spent and crushed. Tamed and used. Sold and bought. There is nothing like it left anywhere, nowhere. It's the last of such buildings standing. The final chapter to a book that has long since gone out of publication.

When will the page be turned? When will we, the readers come to the end? When will the new chapter begin? The one that forms a future of possibility and options; of vibrant and energetic choices.

I open the front door and step inside the house. Perhaps one day I'll find out. Though it'll mean returning to the beginning and re-reading each and every page. Perhaps then I'll know. But I'm not ready yet.

APRIL 2002

I sit beside his brother, trying not to look into his eyes when we talk. It's my first visit to prison. The wide black iron gates open out as he drives the car through into the car-park and leaves it in a parking space, close to the wall at the far end.

The brickwork is dark, shadowed by the large buildings surrounding us from the outside. When the gates close it feels harder to breathe.

We step out of the car and walk over to the front door. Two prison officers in a black uniform show us into a long corridor where we're searched separately and shown into a small side-room, that reminds me of a school dinner hall. The tables and chairs affirm this. Plastic. Only they're nailed down. I imagine the prisoners throwing them at each other in anger if they weren't, shaking my head to rid the next image which forces its way through just as Rowan, wearing a grey sweatshirt and navy jogging trousers walks up to the table where we're seated and plants himself down, hard, against the black chair.

He brings his hand up to hold mine a second longer than necessary and a female prison officer with long dark hair and an annoyed expression painted on her face comes over and shakes her head.

'Do you need anything?'

'No. Got all I need in here. What have you been up too?' he says.

'I come over yours most days after work. I make sure everything's ready for when you come home, read or watch TV, and when it starts getting dark I go home.'

'You haven't seen anyone or been out?' he says.

'No. I won't, not until you get out. It's not the same.'

He smiles.

'You're a good girl, you know that? When I get out we'll have a good time. Just you and me. We'll go away or something,' he says.

'I'll look forward to that.'

Joe shifts in his seat.

'Look after her for me?' he says.

'Sure,' says Joe. 'So how long you got bro?'

'Three months, non-negotiable,' he says.

'Did they find out about Mick?' says Joe.

'I'm no grass. No. And they won't,' he says, looking at me for reassurance.

'No-one will find out anything. It's all gone.'

'What d'you mean?' he says.

'I mean it's gone.'

'Safe?' he says.

I nod. He smiles and then he leans forwards and

kisses my head.

'I miss you,' he says.

'I miss you too.'

'You know I love you, don't you? I'd never see you come to any harm. I want you to keep in touch with Joe. He'll look after you until I get out,' he says, patting his brother on the shoulder.

'I love you too.'

'I'll call her every day,' says Joe, offering Rowan a reassuring smile.

He seems happy with this and stands up from the table, blowing me a kiss as he's lead out of the visiting room by the woman with dark hair.

Back at his I wash the cups and plates I've used, leaving them to drain on the sink and grab the washing from the tumble dryer, heading upstairs to iron his T-shirts. Half an hour later I'm sitting at the dining table with a book when his mobile rings.

I've left it on charge in case anyone needs to get hold of anything. This way I can keep his business going while he's away.

'Hello?'

'Dev, need some stuff Friday,' he says.

'White or brown?'

'White, Four pairs,' he says.

'Be with you Tomorrow.'

'See you then,' he says, before hanging up.

I'll have to get the bus straight after work across town with four grammes of cocaine.

Several minutes pass and the phone rings again. The conversation is much the same. By the third call I've lost interest in my book and slam it down onto the table, losing the page I was on.

Is it going to be this difficult for me to get

things done while he's away?

I take my coat form the hook in the hall and slam the door behind me as I leave the house. It's too much of a good day to waste on sitting in.

APRIL 2015

My second session was today. I meant only to tell Kate of my sunken feeling after the crash. My memories of the dark man and what those memories meant to me. I didn't want to speak of him. Even the thought of his face, those eyes, make my stomach turn. I feel sick to my core. But I have to know why.

I have to go back to that crash and go over that day in minute detail. Just as I'd done with the police. I have to find out what it was that made me jump so easily, what caused my heart to beat harder when I caught sight of a man who spoke and carried himself as that man in the car park did.

I haven't told Koen about my memory lapses and certainly didn't intend to speak of it to Kate either. I think I should though, seeing as the first time it happened had been the day of the crash.

I found myself sat in the same chair as I'd seated myself in before.

The air is cool and the room bright. I made myself comfortable while Kate leafed through my notes. I notice how quiet it is.

'I'm glad you decided to come back,' she says.

'Yes. I'm sure you are.'

I don't mean to sound sarcastic, but I've already told her I'm a therapist and expect her to know that we'll always say that to our clients. I don't want to be patronized.

'So how have things been?'

'Fine. Everything is fine. That's why I don't understand.'

'Understand what?' she says.

'I keep seeing this man. He's shadowed, and he reminds me of the man I saw in the car park before the crash.'

'Oh? I don't remember you mentioning that,' she says.

'I didn't. I didn't know it was relevant until-'

'Until what Marieke?'

She'd not used my name before. Speaking it in a rounded way. The last syllable spoken in a slightly higher tone.

'Until I saw him.'

I see her eyes sparkle, waiting for more information. Curious as to what she could unearth form me.

'I saw a man across the street as I drove up the road the other day. I'd just seen a client, and I wasn't thinking straight. I caught a glimpse of him and immediately thought I recognised him, but I couldn't think where from.'

'I'm concerned at this stage. I'd like to ask you first why you have been continuing to see clients since your supervisor advised you not to do so until you'd completed your eight therapy sessions,' she says, a look of genuine concern spreading across her face.

'I'd already had the session with yourself and I felt safe and comfortable to work with my usual clients. Though I decided not to begin counselling any new clients.'

She shuffles in her chair. I've not seen her appear unsettled before. It strikes me as odd that she is visibly displaying her discomfort to me. Does she do this with her clients? I still can't see myself as one of them. I'm not a client, I am a therapist.

'The man. Do you know him. Do you know who he is?' she says.

Why is she using closed questions? The kind of questions that can only elicit one of two answers, yes or no.

'No. I mean, the man in the car park, no. The man on the street, no. He just reminded me of him.'

'Of who?' she says, looking puzzled.

'The one on the road reminded me of the man in the car park.'

I clench my fingers, holding the faux leather chair tight.

'What was it about him that is holding his image in your mind?' she says.

'I don't know. I thought it was his eyes, but it couldn't have been. I never saw his eyes. It was dark.'

'I'm wondering if they both remind you of someone. A man who you used to know?' she says.

'Yes. They must do. But I've no idea who.'

She considers this a moment before continuing.

'I'd like to try something with you if you will let me. I'm also a qualified hypnotherapist. While I don't see the need at this time to use hypnosis there is a form of self-hypnosis which you can use yourself,' she says.

She stands and walks to a filing cabinet which leans against the wall, beside the small royal blue sofa and passes me some sheets of paper.

'On here you will find some exercises. They teach you deep relaxation skills where you can still your mind. I want to show you first how it's done and then you can continue yourself at home,' she says.

'I understand how visualisation works.'

She continues without acknowledgement.

'First. I'd like you to make yourself comfortable. Breathe deeply and still your mind and just listen to the words as I speak. Try not to think. If you find yourself thinking just accept the words or pictures your mind offers you and let them pass through and out. Can you do that for me?' she says.

I put the sheets of paper onto the floor and force my hands to relax, letting them fall in my lap.

'I'll try.'

I lean back into the chair, close my eyes and listen. Then she begins.

'I am taking you on a journey. We are going to the place where you are happiest. Where you feel safe. This is your space. I want you to imagine you are walking through an archway. The air is still and warm. The place is quiet and peaceful. You are calm and content. You are going to walk through the archway and when you come out the other side you will be there, in your special place. Your safe place. A space for you, and you know what this place is, what it looks like.'

I find myself at the other end of an archway, coated in fuscia coloured roses. The sun is light, the sky is blue, and the air is warm, just as she says.

I walk slowly at first, taking in my surroundings and breathing in the scent of fresh cut flowers. My pace quickens when I turn the corner.

The garden ends suddenly and I find myself beside a large waterfall. The water is cascading down in troths and sloshing about in the river below. I feel edgy but I don't know why.

I continue past the sounds of rushing water, filling at the bottom where it dips and stills, surrounded by stones. At the edge of the lane I look up and see a bridge.

I want to stand on the bridge. To see the scenery from above. I edge closer and find clean stone steps which appear as if from nowhere. I take them, one at a time to the top where I find myself ten feet above the water.

I'm usually scared stiff of heights but up here I feel safe. I walk to the middle of the bridge and as I stand, looking out at the water I catch a glimpse of colour. When I turn I find that it's clothing. I follow the colours up to his face.

He's standing a few feet away from me, then he

is behind me. Then just as suddenly he stands beside me. He lifts his arm out and offers me his hand. I take it, somehow knowing that I'm safe with him. Knowing that this faceless, peace-giving being is there for me. He doesn't say anything but I hear him speak to me, 'it's okay, you're safe now.'

I hear sobbing. Light, gentle sobbing. Someone is crying. It's only when I feel a tissue in my hand that I remember where I am.

'You can open your eyes,' she says.

I do. I raise my head and meet Kate's eyes. She looks concerned and gentle.

'Would you like to tell me what caused you to feel sad?' she says.

'No. I'm not sad. I don't know what I feel but it isn't sad. Happy? I felt so safe. When he came to the bridge I felt as though nothing could hurt me, nothing could touch me.'

'I'm interested in your choice of words. What did you think would make you hurt? Who is going to touch you?' she asks.

'I don't know. All I know is that he came and held my hand and I felt so calm and safe.'

'Is this the man you said you saw? The one you thought you saw, I wonder?' she asks.

'No. I don't think so. I don't know.'

'Well do you know who this safe man is?' she asks.

'No. I don't know him either. He's like a God.'

I'm just as surprised by this comment as Kate seems to be.

'Are you religious Marieke?' she says.

'No. I'm not. In fact religion is alien to me.'

I can't help laughing. I'm not the kind of person to go all spiritual. But it makes sense to me that this man, his image is God-like. He's safe to be around and he protects me.

I think back to a book I read once, about angels and remember the image of Archangel Michael. He stands tall with a sword at his side, protecting all who ask for his help. Had I asked for his help? Was it he who had come to me?

'Do you recognise him?' she says.

This question seems strange but I answer as honestly as I can.

'Yes. Though I can't think where from. I thought at first it was from a book, the Archangel Michael. But then he looks different. His appearance is normal. In yet he has the feel of someone other-worldly. No, that's not the right word. He has the energy of someone not of this earth, of a higher being. But he looks just like any other man.

'Can you describe him to me?' she says.

'He's got dark hair. I can't see his face but I know he's smiling. He's tall and sturdy, like a tree. An oak tree, strong and protective.'

'I wonder, do you have a partner?' she says.

Of course that's not on the consultation form.

'Yes. I'm married actually.'

'What does your husband look like?' she says.

I stop and take in her question, analysing the importance of it.

'He's tall and well built with dark hair.'

She smiles. A knowing smile. I smile too, realising the significance of this description.

'It's him, isn't it?'

'Is it?' she says.

'Yes. I think so.'

'What can you take away from here today?' she says.

'My husband is my protector. I feel safe with him. He's looking after me. He always has been.'

She smiles then her expression falters.

'What do you mean?' she says.

I hadn't told her I'd seen the man on the bridge before. I remember him from a dream or day-dream. A thought, an image, a picture in my mind, from a long time ago. Though I still can't remember the first time I saw him. The first time he came to me. I don't know when, where or why. I just know that he's always been there for me and that the very first time I saw him I'd been glad. Glad that he was my saviour, a part of my past. But that was before I'd even met Koen.

'I've seen him before. I remember the man on the bridge. It was before I met Koen.'

Kate glances at the clock and I follow her gaze, noticing we're coming to the end of our session. I don't want to go over so I decide to allow her to end the session.

'I know we have to conclude for today, but I'll be back next week, and I'll give these a go.'

I bend down and pick up the sheets from the floor. I'm so used to giving homework to my own clients that it seems strange to be taking some back to do myself.

'Is there anything you need to air before you leave?' she says.

'No. I'll get on with these and I'll see you next week.'

I smile as I leave the room and close the door

behind me.

I collect Alice from school on the way home. Back inside the familiar, cosy surroundings of our house I feel better knowing that the man on the bridge has been there all along, looking out for me, and that he always will be. I'll do the visualisation exercises, which I know more of than she assumes. Being a stress management specialist I've used them with my own clients many times, I've just never felt the need to practice them myself.

Koen arrives back from work just as I'm dishing up. I set the plates of food down on the dining table as he comes into the room.

'Smells nice,' he says.

Pulling out the chair I catch him glancing at the food he's been presented with and then at me.

'How'd it go today then?' he says.

'Fine. Actually she's given me some meditation exercises to do. I think our first session worked, not that I'm stressed. It just helps to unwind.'

'I think I could do with some of that,' he says, tucking in to his dinner.

There is something about such simple acts of living which make my heart swell with satisfaction and pride. Proud that I've found such an old fashioned man to share mine and my daughters life with. One who shows us love, support, and a laid-back confidence that no matter what the problem we'll always be able to work through it, together. And content in knowing it will always be this way. I love every inch of him. I could watch him all day, pottering around, eating. Just normal everyday things people take for granted, but that I take note of.

When I'm walking I'm in a rush, speeding past everything. I find the practice meditative. Perhaps I should leave the car at home tomorrow and walk in to work, slow my pace a bit. Whilst walking fast allows me to tune out, maybe it's time I started tuning in, feeling the ground beneath my feet and centering myself.

'You alright love? You look miles away?' he says.

'Yes. I was just thinking I'll walk to work tomorrow, get some fresh air.'

'Good idea,' he says.

As I prepare the pudding and wash the dishes he comes up behind me and nestles his head between my shoulder and neck.

'Let me finish those. Go sit yourself down. We'll have an early night and cuddle up on the sofa with a film,' he says.

I leave him to it and walk into the living room, finding he's already planned the night. A film already sits in the DVD player and a box of chocolates have been left on the coffee table.

Settling down beneath a blanket I rest my head on Koen's chest. Half way through the film something clicks. The woman is running from something. Her hair sweeps past her face and the shadow of whoever or whatever is chasing her flits past a tree. In the woods she's trying to get away. Trying to find a way out. She trips and falls. Her hair now soaked with perspiration, sticking to the skin of her forehead. The thing is moving between the trees, behind her. She can't get up in time. It pounces.

That's when it clicks. The sound becomes muffled. The picture distorted. The woman's breath,

I can hear over everything else. Loud, as though she's in the room with me. I want to tell her to run. I want to grab her, take her hand, pull her out of there and run with her. I want to get her to safety. I want to scream, but when I open my mouth nothing will come out, not a sound.

I open and close my mouth several times. I feel my throat tighten. I can't breathe. For a few moments I'm scared. I feel the woman's fear. The woman is me, and it frightens me. Her face comes up close to mine. I hear her whisper as she turns her head and leans in close to my ear.

'Scream quietly or they'll hear.'

I jump up from the curve in the sofa. Where I fit snug between the back of the head-rest and his body. I stand and walk to the kitchen.

My throat burns with the tightness. My chest is crushing. Like a lead weight is pressing against my rib cage. I gasp for breath as if I've just come up for air from a dive in the sea. I lean against the worktop. My hands gripping the edge of the sink.

Now I've left the room the woman is gone. Her image has left me. Her words have left my thoughts. In fact I have none. I don't think. I can't think. I want to scream and shout and cry but I've no idea why. No idea what it was that set me off, what triggered this feeling. This inescapable feeling of dread, impending doom. I feel scared and I want to run. I feel trapped and constrained but I'm aware that I can leave at any time. I'm not a prisoner. I haven't been kidnapped. But that's what it feels like.

The reality in which I find myself contradicts the feelings I have within me. My body doesn't agree with the situation I'm in. It's as though my skin is a film, separating me from the outside. Where the danger is I don't know. It seems to be within me, rather than external.

Everything, the walls, the ceiling, the doors, my own hands are distorted. Fuzzy and fake. My body is disconnected from my head. I watch my arms reach out. My hands grab a glass of water from the side. Filling it up and bringing it to my lips. I feel the water sliding down my throat. My thirst is quenched. My heart still pounding I watch as I walk out of the kitchen and back into the living room.

I continue to sense her near. The woman, throughout the film. I can smell the leaves and hear the mud squelching beneath her bare feet as she runs from the woods and is eventually caught in the arms of her attacker. A film separates me from the world. I'm standing back, watching. Listening and observing. Not really here but aware of everything else that is.

When the film ends koen is asleep. I don't want to wake him so I pull the blanket up close to his face and turn the TV off. Leaving the lamp on for him, I make my way upstairs. I cross the landing and see Alice asleep, in a star position on the bed. I close her bedroom door gently and turn, heading to my own.

I undress mechanically. Slip a night-gown on and slide beneath the covers. I gaze at the ceiling until I cannot hold my eyes open a second longer. I feel them heavy and achingly close. I hear my breathing slow and steady. The stillness in the house clouds over the noises of the day and I sink into a deep, narcotic glaze. A sleep much deeper than I have had in months.

I awake, still tired, to the soothing chirp of birds nesting in the tree a few feet from the window. I stand smaller this morning. My feet light and weak. I rub my eyes clear and see an image of the girl flash across them. It lasts only a few seconds but I know that it's her. She's lying in a pool of blood. The mud has given way to carpet. Thick cream carpet.

The rest of the day passes in a blur. This is one of those times where you feel as though you have not slept at all. Where you feel that you could just curl up anywhere and rest your eyes, sleep for eternity.

Snippets of conversation and sessions with clients are a haze of fog. A mist that clears slowly and does not disappear entirely. By evening I cannot keep my eyes open any longer and skip dinner to lay down on the bed upstairs.

Koen joins me a while later. I feel the bed dip. He rests his head against the pillow and edges closer to me, his face inches from my head. His breath warm and tingling on my neck. He wraps me in his arms and holds me close. His legs against mine. The skin of his chest against the silk of my night-gown.

He kisses me gently. My neck first, and then nibbles the lower part of my ear. My cheek, then my throat. He looks up at me but I have already gone. I can feel nothing but see and hear everything. He removes my knickers and his boxers. Slowly, seductively. He raises my right leg with his own and brings his entire body to rest against mine. My back to him, I can't see him. I can't see his face, his eyes. As he holds my leg apart with his hand I jolt forward. My body stiffens, my chest tight. The crushing of my lungs and the sickness burst through my chest and stomach as I feel my heart race. I can't breathe. I can't hear. I can only see, and I can't see him.

I jump from the bed and run from the room. By the time he's lifted himself up from the bed I've made it to the bathroom. Lost in a haze, not knowing where the door is, I can't find my way out. The door swings open and it's him. His face. His eyes. The way he stands. The tone and pitch of his voice. He's found me. He's come for me. I can't escape. What is he going to do?

I stand frozen in the corner of the bathroom, between the sink and the bath. He walks right up to me and holds me. Holds me close. Rubs the hair on the back of my head as though soothing an injured dog. I breathe in as though for the first time. Until now I have been choked. I catch the slightest hint of musk. Some aftershave I don't recognise. I look up, not wanting to but knowing I have to and find the room has returned to normal.

The bathroom I had only seconds before been stood in is painted turquoise. Shells drape from the ceiling from trips to the beach. Holidays in the sun. The floor is laminated, not linoleum.

'Are you alright?' he asks.

His eyes are chestnut with a speck of jade. His hair is dark. His frame large. He wears no tattoo's on his arms. He wears genuine concern and curiosity on his face.

He lets me go. His hands until now have been holding my shoulders. He stands back.

'What are you scared of?' he asks.

'I don't know. I thought I was somewhere else. The door had moved. I wanted to get out.'

'What do you mean the door had moved?' he asks.

'It wasn't where it should be. Where I saw it.'

'Why did you want to get out?' he asks, his face a picture of confusion.

'I thought I was trapped. I wanted to escape. You were someone else.'

'Who did you think I was?'

'Another man. He had light hair and blue eyes. I don't know who he is or what he wants but he won't leave me alone.'

I can't help myself. The pain is almost too much to bear. It fills my core and spreads down my legs and up to my chest. A dull ache that thickens and grips me as though it's a physical pain. In a few moments it will pass as it always does and I'll return to my usual self. But right now it feels as though it will take me over. Control me, destroy me, consume me. I know it won't but I can't make the feeling go away and so I try to ride with it. Breathe through the terror as it unfolds.

Koen holds me while I cry. The release of tears I am unprepared for. They spill from my eyes and spread down my face like raindrops. I don't feel sad. I feel angry; with myself for looking so stupid, for appearing so weak. Crying like an emotional woman. Like a hysteric. Like a crazy person.

Koen takes my hand and leads me from the bathroom and down the stairs.

'Would you like a cupa?' he says.

I nod my head. A few minutes later he returns

from the kitchen with two cups and passes me mine while he sits on the sofa. I seat myself next to him. My legs together, facing slightly away from him.

'What happened just now, was that some kind of flashback?' he says.

I knew what they were. I knew how to treat them and still I didn't want to believe that was what was happening to me. A traumatised therapist.

'I think so.'

'You must know. You must have some idea where all this is coming from?' he says.

MAY 2002

Lee was standing at the door when I opened it. He looked as though he was expecting something.

'D'you need anything? Only I'm on my way out.'

'No. Actually I wondered if you had a minute,' he says.

'I can't let you in.'

'Okay. I'm sure Rowan won't mind. I just wanted to talk to you, that's all,' he says, pulling his arm up and ruffling the back of his head with his hand.

'Is it important?'

'Not exactly, well I guess it depends-'

'Come in.'

I sit on the edge of the chair, closest to the window in the living room. Though he's in prison and won't be out for a while I still feel calmer knowing that if he did walk up the drive I'd have seen him and will have time to get rid of Lee.

'So what did you want to talk to me about?'

'It's a bit personal. Tell me to mind my own

122

business but...,Amanda said she...,is Rowan violent?' he says, looking right into my eyes.

'No. Never.'

'I said she was worrying over nothing but you know some women can...,well you know-'

'Why did she think that?'

'She saw some bruises. She said he must have done it. She said she saw the way he looked at you sometimes and I must admit-'

'You thought so too?'

He nods and looks down at his feet like a scorned child.

'I've got to say though that sometimes he is out of order. Always holding onto you as if he's scared to let go, in case you leave. There is something, but I can't put my finger on it,' he says.

'How long have you known him?'

'Since college,' he says. 'But that's it. He's changed since he met you. He went a bit off the wall when his ex left him but he got over it quickly. When he met you he just...,oh I don't know. He seems more serious.'

'And that's a bad thing?'

'It is for him. We used to have a laugh. Now he's messing about with drugs and...the boxing used to come first you know-'

'So it's my fault? Since we met he's let himself go. Is that it?'

'No. That's not what I'm saying-'

'I've got to go now. I don't think you should come here while he's away.'

When he stands and makes his way over to the door he turns and looks me in the eye again.

'He doesn't like you having friends does he?' he

says.

'I've got friends-'

'Male friends. That's why you want me to leave,' he says.

'You're not my friend. You're his.'

'If you do ever need anything, let me know. It doesn't matter what time of day or night. If there's something going on, it isn't right,' he says.

I should have said, 'I'll never need you,' but instead I asked him 'how will I get hold of you?'

'Is this yours?' he asks, grabbing my phone from the small table.

I nod. He taps in his number.

'I've saved it under Amanda. Change the name if you need to. If I get a call from anyone I don't recognise it goes straight to voicemail. It's a new phone so Rowan doesn't have this number,' he says, handing me back my mobile.

I should have deleted it. I should have told him I'd never need to call him. I should have changed the name. There's lot's of things I should have done but I didn't, And I'm glad I didn't.

MAY 2015

It's lighter in the evenings now that summer is soon to arrive. I see the fresh blossom bursting and a few petals fall down my back as I walk beneath the trees. I look across the road and see a couple walking hand in hand.

There's something about the way they walk that attracts my attention. They look as though they're in a bubble. Alone, together in the world. Why are they up so early? More to the point why am I?

I haven't been sleeping well. My dreams are vivid and I wake up believing I am there, in that house. The one with the Fleur-de-Lys wallpaper. I never get to see his face but that man is haunting me. He's in my dreams, in my waking thoughts. He wears the same clothes each time, denim blue jeans and a white T-shirt with black leather boots.

I sometimes think I'm loosing my mind. No. I know I'm not. Mad people don't know they're mad. I just can't get him out of my head. He's more real now. Almost like flesh and blood. Like a real living person. Someone I once knew or saw as I crossed the street. I know his eyes are blue. Deep and soulful, piercing azure.

I shake my head in my sleep. Koen told me. He said that when I moan and thrash around in bed my head rocks from side to side. I know he's right. I wake up with a sore neck.

I try not to think of that now. I have a session with Heather this morning and I don't want to project my crap onto her.

In the therapy room I notice something has shifted. When I ask her about it she clams up. She shows this by drawing her shoulders up and in so that her neck disappears.

'Can you tell me any more about this feeling?'

'It comes in waves. Sometimes I don't even know I'm doing it. Sometimes I do. Like the other day in the supermarket. There was this man. He knocked into me, by accident. He said he was sorry, but, I don't know...,' she says, gazing down at her feet and then lifting her head back to meet my eyes.

'Then what happened?'

'I froze. Fear or shock or...,I don't know. I froze. That's all I know,' she says.

'Can I ask what you mean by, 'that's all I know,' Did you do something afterwards?'

'I can't remember. I don't remember coming home and going to bed, let alone leaving the shop,' she says.

That familiar churning begins in my stomach, like a cement mixer. Churning and spinning. I feel sick.

'Excuse me,' I say, running from the room and

up the staircase to the bathroom.

I return to the consulting room and apologise, tell her I have got a sickness bug. That I will see her next week. I can't wait to leave. I lock the doors quick and travel home as fast as I legally can.

When I get there Koen is asleep on the sofa. It's his day off. I creep across the living room to get the phone.

I know it's time. It's time to take my own therapy seriously. No more relaxation. No more visualisation. No more talking over and skirting around the issue. It's time to face up to this. Whatever this is.

When Heather looses herself, looses touch with reality, I want to say to her, 'you're dissociating. You've suffered an unimaginable trauma. Something so terrible happened that you forgot. You have stored away the event somewhere deep within your mind, and now that you're older and wiser, willing and ready, you're better equipped to deal with it. Your brain knows this and wants you to remember. You have to talk about it. Get it out. Throw the words at me so that we can deal with it together. You're strong enough to do that now.'

Now it seems that I may be doing the same thing. I have to find out. I have to know, who that man is and why he's haunting me.

Since he came along all I've done is try to pretend, try not to think about it. But it won't go away. He won't go away until I face him, and find out what it is he wants to say.

I dial the number and speak to the receptionist. I don't tell her why, just that it's urgent. I need to speak to Kate as soon as possible. I throw in that I'm a colleague of hers, hoping that this will stop the receptionist from feeling sorry for me. I want her to know that I'm just as qualified, if not more so, than Kate.

An hour passes. Koen has woken up and finds me in the kitchen, leaning with my back against the cupboards.

'You OK? You look pale?' he says.

'I'm fine. There's just something I need to do. I'm waiting for a call any minute.'

'A client?' he says.

I wonder if I should tell him. I think of an excuse but decide not to bother. He will see through me. I may as well be honest.

'Actually I'm the client. I need to speak to Kate. There's something I need to get off my chest.'

I flick the switch and wait for the kettle to boil. It's only as I pour myself a cup of coffee that he speaks again.

'Is this about the other night?' he says.

I can't think what he means. He must see the confusion in my face because he comes closer and puts his hands on my hips. Pulling me in to him.

'You know I'm here for you don't you? For both of you,' he says, tilting his head towards the open door which leads to the hallway where Alice is smashing toy cars into one another on the carpet.

'I know you are. This is just something I have to do myself, for now.'

'OK,' he says. But don't forget I love you.'

As he nears the stairs I realise it's too late to ask him what he meant about 'the other night.' Still, I reason it can't be that important otherwise he would have asked me more.

I sit with the cup of steaming coffee between my hands. I grow bored and switch the radio on. A love song bursts from the speakers. Gentle and hypnotic. A soulful voice.

I'm temporarily transported back to our engagement party. The laughter and joy of our friends welcoming the young couple, declaring their promise to marry each other, to spend their lives together.

I see the fabric of my silk dress, shorter than I remember it being. Swirling and dancing as though it's a second skin. My legs stick thin and pale against the rich peach. It feels expensive. It looks expensive. Suddenly I'm floating. No longer to the beat of the music, but instead I'm high up on the ceiling somewhere, watching myself dance. I can see the top of my head and my nose. A glint of sparkle coming from a thin chain of gold around my neck. A diamond ring on my finger. Not the one I know. Not the one I've worn on my finger since the day I said yes.

I'm free. Flying. Soaring above myself, looking down on everyone. I don't recognise any of the faces. Just as I catch myself take a sip from the glass which is placed in front of me I catch the side of Koen's face. Except it's not Koen. It's someone else. It's him. The man in jeans, the one with the boots. I force myself to look down and there I see them, black. I look up to meet his face and it's his eyes I see first. Blue. His hair is golden, blonde. He looks at me and smiles for a few seconds and it takes me a while to respond. I smile back at him. But it doesn't look right. It seems forced. He leans closer, whispers something in my ear and his face changes. His features alter. His eyes steel, his lips clasped tightly together, his cheeks thin. He looks tense. Frustrated.

I let go of his hand and turn to walk away. I open the door and tread the thick cream carpet to the stairs. It's at this point that I feel a deep unsettling sensation fill me. Anticipation and dread. I don't know what's going to happen but I know that it's not right. I know I can't look any further. I want to grab her hand and drag her to the front door. I want to take her and run. I don't know why.

As suddenly as I was sent into this daylight dream I'm taken from it. The music has ended. The weather is being discussed. I move to switch the radio off and as I do so the telephone sings from my hand. I answer it as soon as I regain the function of my fingers. Which now feel as though I'm no longer in control of. My hand is clenched over the receiver, my fingers white with the strain.

'Hello.'

It's Kate returning my call. She says she will see me tomorrow as she has just had a cancellation. I tell her enough to make her aware that I need to speak with her sooner rather than later and that it's got something to do with the crash, but I don't reveal any more over the phone. I know only too well what it's like taking a call from a client after work and how it often interferes in your family time when you do.

I feel a little reassured from my recent snippet of a memory, but also more perplexed. Why is this happening to me? What could it all mean?

Until recently I was a normal wife and mother, a counsellor and enjoying life. My job made me happy, my husband made me smile, my daughter made me laugh and together I was whole. I still smile. I still laugh, but I no longer feel whole.

Is this what they call transference? Am I allowing my clients, particularly Heather, to project their feelings and spoken thoughts onto me? Am I just exhibiting the physiological and psychological symptoms of a woman who was abused as a child? Or is this some form of burn-out? Have I reached a point in my career where I am doing more harm to my clients than good? Taking on board all their problems. Bringing home their issues and experiencing them as my own?

I remember everything except the important events in life. Births, marriages, deaths, are all gone, deleted from my mind as though they never were. I can't remember those years. When we met or married, the holiday in Cornwall with our friends, my daughters father. I can't picture him; his face or his body close to mine. I don't remember anything special from the past thirteen years.

What I do remember is Kate's number. It's etched into my mind, like a salve or a medicinal drug. A safety net.

I clean this house from top to bottom myself and not once can I remember coming across any photographs. The only ones that I've seen are visible to everyone. In frames on the mantle-piece or on the wall leading up the stairs, pictures of us three, smiling at the camera in a pose. Presented to appear as any normal family in a studio, though I can't remember where. They're all of the same day, whenever that was. I'm wearing a black V-neck dress, cut off just above the knee. Alice wears a pink fluffy jumper beneath blue denim dungaree's. Koen wears an egg blue T-shirt and dark navy jeans. His hair is thicker, slightly spiked at the top, cut back at the sides. My hair is longer and light. It must have been summer. Alice looks around four. Three years ago. She smiles, but her face looks worried. I'm anxious. That I can tell from the way I force my head to the side to look at Koen as he stares at the camera. His expression is neutral. His posture perfect. We all look as though our minds are elsewhere.

I forget to say goodbye to Koen. He calls out as I leave but I don't catch his words.

I'm still thinking about those photographs as I turn the corner and walk towards the therapy centre. I can't get those pictures out of my mind. It's like a wall has been built between me and those faces of myself I don't recognise.

I wonder if I've stored or forgotten anything. Are there any photographs up in the loft? Do I have any shoe-boxes filled with old letters or diaries?

I know I kept them years ago. I can remember writing in a journal when I was around eleven years old, about what me and my friends had got up to during the school holidays. Where were they now? I can't remember the last time I met up with any of my family either. They were always too busy. After the wedding I saw less and less of mine and more of his. It was the same with our friends. Mine began dwindling away. Moving on, getting married, having children while I remained a housewife and concentrated on taking care of Alice.

I remember most of the pregnancy, the birth and even being alone with Alice but I only have vague recollections of her father. A drunken one-night stand. A bit of fun that left me carrying a child I wasn't sure how to look after alone.

I did it though. I managed it well. But it was not enough. That's when I became interested in the mind, mental health and how to support people through difficult times. I went to college, obtained a diploma and set up my own practice. I worked with women only for a long time. Koen said it would be easier, and he was right. He's always right. He seems to understand me. He knows how I tick, sometimes more than myself.

There seems to be a distant part of me that does remember him, Alice's father, but the other half of me doesn't want to. Perhaps that's because of Koen. Perhaps it's because he's such a wonderful father and a loving husband I've wiped that part of my life clear from my head. After-all, what kind of a man takes on another mans child, only to be thought of as the step-father or the one who bothered. No, he wants to be known as her father and that is a promise I made long ago. Alice would call Koen dad and know no other man as her father. That man, whoever he was has never been a part of her life and never will. I'll never tell her and I hope that Koen respects that decision.

What else can I remember? I must surely think this over if Kate ever asks me or if anyone ever questions me over something. I must be able to tell them who I am, what I've done and relive with my grand-children if Alice ever has any and they ever ask me, my happiest memories.

I have to work. It's the only thing I know how to do. It's the only piece of the jigsaw that fits right now. I'm aware of my credentials. I remember learning, college and study groups. I remember choosing to do it, but not why. Or at what point I thought I would make a good therapist.

I near the turn in the road and make my way over to the building. Heather is waiting for me. Leaning against the wall with a cigarette in her hand.

'I know I'm early but I had to see you before we went in. I think I remember something,' she says.

'Let's go inside and talk there.'

Once inside she takes a seat in the corner of the room, drops her handbag on the floor beside the chair and shuffles out of her coat, leaving it draping across the arm of the chair.

'I know this sounds odd but I've realised something. Something important,' she says.

I have not had a chance to sit yet and do not want her to feel as though I am taking control of the conversation by standing so I sit down quickly. A pain shoots up my back as I do and I realise I have put my back out again. I have been struggling with sciatica for years. Again I cannot remember when it began or for how long it has affected me.

She starts before I have the chance to ask her to.

'Last night I realised something. I suppose I knew all along but I just couldn't verbalise it before. I had a boyfriend in school. He was a bit older than me. Actually he went to college. He was training as a mechanical engineer. He was charming and sweet, but hiding something. A bad boy, ya know? Anyway, he was quite a catch. Deep brown eyes and wavy hair. I fell for him. It was alright for a few months, then he started getting a bit possessive, ya know? Calling all the time, checking up on me, asking where I'd been. In the end I'd had enough. It was after I'd left him that he hit me.'

'I never saw him again but I heard he was a violent bloke and had connections, ya know? There was something on the telly about grooming the other day and I thought, that's him. The type, ya know? All smiles and compliments, controlling, possessive, then violent and abusive. He was grooming me in a way wasn't he? And I let him. I only left when I felt the heat of danger I was in. What if I'd have stayed? Would I still be here?' she says, spinning a piece of hair between her fingers.

I shift in my chair. That uncomfortable feeling in the pit of my stomach starts again.

'I was drinking a lot when we were together, and my father wasn't the nicest of men either. I couldn't tell him. Maybe I didn't block it out. Maybe it was my age, the drink. Ya know?'

'Yes I do know. Will you excuse me one moment.'

I keep my composure until I leave the room and as soon as the door is closed behind me, the click of the latch in place, I crumble. Sink to the floor and drop like a ton of lead weight. I've been holding this weight for so long that I can't continue. I have to let it go. But how?

There is a time, a place, where you will find yourself. A day, a moment, when you will step back and consider the meaning of life. Your own life. You will question why we're here. Wonder why we have hurt and lost, loved and found. This is my moment.

I notice the curve of the ring on my index finger, made by the heat of my skin. I watch the birds fly and soar in groups up over the wall and pass me as I watch from the window, gliding towards the rooftop. I notice the stains on the fence outside next to the wall. The rust on the car. Everything is stained. Dirty, broken, tainted. Like my life, like me.

I'm ruined, an empty shell. I exist only because I was not brave enough or clever enough to complete suicide. I'm here. Awake, alive, breathing. For what? What's my purpose? Why am I here? Why am I alive?

I walk to the end of the road and fall in pace with the footsteps I hear behind me. When I notice them I jump. An elderly woman steps back and walks around me, never leaving my gaze. She's watching me. They all are. They're all staring at me or right through me. Everyone does it. Like I don't mean anything at all. Like I don't exist.

Perhaps I don't. Perhaps I'm not really here. Maybe I died long ago and my ghost still walks the streets, still goes about the daily chores, still sleeps in a bed with a man I only vaguely remember marrying. Is it an illusion? A dream, a nightmare? Is this heaven? Is my sleep reality?

I cross the road and make it to the other side avoiding becoming trapped beneath the car that speeds past me and races around the corner as I step up on to the pavement. A car pulls up on the curb. A middle-aged man steps out, a woman beside him. They both wear jeans and T-shirts. CID, I notice straight away.

'Where are you going?' says the man.

'Out.'

'You've been hurt. Who did this to you?' he says.

The woman beside him nods and steps forwards while he steps back.

'I'm Karen. A CID officer. We're investigating someone. Are you injured?' she asks, stepping forwards to examine my face.

I step back and onto the mans feet.

'Sorry. I'm going out. You'll have to excuse me.'

'We want to help. If you've been a victim of a crime then you really should get some medical attention-'

'And then do what? Have pictures taken? Make a statement? I haven't been a victim of anything and I don't want to talk to you.'

The woman passes me a card.

'Call us if you need anything. We're only up the road,' she says.

I stuff the card in my jacket pocket and continue walking.

The man calls out to me as I pass the bus stop. A group of teenagers sit huddled at one end smoking a joint. The smell wafts through the air. I am surprised the police did not smell it.

'We're looking for someone. A man,' he says, running back to meet me at the corner near the crossing.

'I don't know anyone round here.'

'You might know this man,' he says. 'His name is

Rowan Marsen. He lives-'

'I know him. What do you want?'

'He's wanted in connection with a serious assault. In fact it's a little worse than that. He lives on that road,' he says, pointing back up to the road I have just left.

I didn't want to go back, but I had to show him where Rowan lived.

As I turn the corner to show the CID officer the road I find myself lost. The road is unrecognisable. The street is smaller than I remember. I can't find the house. The numbers are wrong. I hear the sound of a woman's voice in the background.

'Jack, come on, this is not good. We'll find it love,' she says.

The mans face has changed, distorted. His features have altered. He's no longer the CID officer but a young man with a wife and two children in a double buggy beside him. They huff and stroll away, continuing to look at the numbers of the houses as they pass. Whatever they're hoping to find or whoever they're looking for it's in this time, the present, where I am.

Is this the first time I've slipped? Is this the first time I've lost reality in a public place? Blanked out, dissociated.

I hope it isn't but know it is. It's dangerous. It's much too dangerous to be leaving your own skin like that near a road.

I stand a few moments, shaking and make my way back to the house. I have to go home. A hot bath and a mug of coffee will return me to my present self. I'm sure it will. I hope it will.

There's only one problem when I reach the gate

and go to step back inside, the front door has been left open. I call out to Koen but there's no answer. I run up to Alice's room, but it's empty. Where are they? They were here only minutes ago.

I run back down the stairs to the kitchen, check the garden. See through the window that the car is still parked in the driveway. What the fuck?

'Looking for someone?' says a woman, peeping from behind the hedge of next doors garden.

'Yes. My husband. The doors been left open. I can't find him or my daughter.'

'You won't find anyone in there love. Nobody lives there any more,' she says.

'What do you mean, this is my house.'

'I don't think so,' she laughs. 'Take a look,' she says.

I turn and notice the windows at the top of the house are boarded up. The door is not white UPVC but white painted wood. The car on the drive is the same make and model, colour as well, but the car seat is not in the back and the wheel-trims and registration plate are wrong. I look back down the street and see him climbing up the curve of the road with a rucksack on his back.

He smiles and winks as he passes me. He gives me that look too. That look of a living person coming across a ghost for the first time. A look of wonderment and curiosity.

'I don't understand.'

'Are you alright? Here let me help you,' she says.

The woman half walks, half carries me from the house and over to the other side of the road. I don't want to go. I don't want to look.

'Do you recognise this street?' she says.

I nod in agreement.

'Did you used to know somebody who lived here?' she says.

'Yes.'

'Who?' she says.

'A man.'

'What was his name?' she says.

'Rowan.'

The woman takes both my shoulders in her arms and looks me in the eye.

'What happened to him Marieke?' she says.

'How do you know my name?'

'What happened to Rowan?' she says.

'I don't know. I left him. I walked out.'

'No Marieke. He found you. You came back. What did you do to him?' she says, her eyes piercing my very thoughts.

'I never came back-'

'We've always wondered what happened here all those years ago. You don't remember me do you?' she says.

'No, I don't. Let go of me.'

I turn and run back down the road, away from that house, away from her. But as I turn the corner and step back onto the pavement beside the main road I look back and that's when I remember.

JUNE 2002

I walk along the street, opposite the pub and turn right. The road curves into a cul-de-sac and straight ahead sits a small house, converted into a ground-floor and first floor flat. I walk up to the door and knock.

'Come in,' Amanda says, smiling.

'Thanks for inviting me.'

'No problem. A friend of Rowans is a friend of ours,' she says.

I follow her on through the large hallway and down some steps into a conservatory. The doors are open and a light breeze filters through from the garden. I can smell the burgers before I see them cooking on the BBQ on the side of the patio where four chairs and a plastic table sit, right in the sun.

'What would you like, says Lee, flipping over some sausages, while he sips cold beer from a glass in his other hand.

'I wouldn't mind one of those first.'

He passes me a bottle and a glass and starts whistling to himself.

'So how is everything?' she says.

'Fine. Just waiting for Rowan to come home.'

'How long is it?' she says.

'He'll be out next month.'

She smiles but she can't stop the brief worry which flits past her face and leaves a slight frown. Noticing me watching her she turns away and asks Lee where the salad is.

'I'll get it.'

I walk into the kitchen and grab the bowl. As I place it onto the table and turn around to jump back in my seat I see them exchange a glance.

'Is there something wrong?'

'No. I just don't feel well that's all,' she says, bending down to cradle her slightly swollen stomach.

'Is it the baby? You should get yourselves off to the hospital. We'll do this another day.'

'It's probably nothing,' she says.

'Then it won't matter if you bother them then will it?'

'Go on. I'll clear this up and lock up after you.'

Amanda looks to Lee for support and he places his arm across her back and walks out the door with her.

'Eat some of that food to save it going to waste. Lee will come and pick up the keys later,' she says bending over as another cramp takes over.

I finish the bottle of beer and take another from the table. I don't feel like eating so I wrap the burgers up in cling-film and leave them in the fridge. I lock the door as I leave and send a silent prayer up to whoever is listening, hoping the baby is okay, and that Amanda is well.

Lee arrives later to collect the keys. He's been crying and I'm in half a mind to offer him a hug of comfort but I hear Rowan's warning and step back before I do.

'Do you need anything? Does Amanda need anything?'

'No. Thanks for locking up and putting the BBQ away,' he says.

'No worries.'

'See you soon,' he says, turning away in time to catch a falling tear.

I've never seen a grown man cry with genuine sadness and it strikes me harder than if Amanda were standing in front of me doing the same thing.

'I'm here if you, either of you need anything okay.'

'You too,' he says firmly.

I nod and walk back into the house.

Later as I sip from a glass of cool white wine I think back to the baby we lost, a little girl, and wonder why we have to bear such silent pain. Why do women never talk of miscarriage as though it's some dirty little secret?

I shake my head to rid the images which threaten to creep up on me. I can't think of that now. I have to get everything ready for when he comes home.

JUNE 2015

I wake up with a heavy head. Drowsy, disorientated. The dream felt so real. I was being held down. My wrists pressed into the mattress. My heart pounding against his. I shake my head to rid the image of his face pressed against mine. His eyes deep set searching my mind. The weight of his chest and elbows digging into my skin. Grinding me down. Damp, sweat and tears. Mine and his.

I lift myself up from the bed. My shorts stick to me. A stain on the sheets. I've pissed myself. I walk in to the bathroom and toss the dirty clothes into the laundry basket and run the hot tap. Lathering the shower gel into the sponge, I scrub myself down and try not to think. It's easier not to think. Clear my mind and pretend I don't know why I want to feel the boiling water run over my skin, melting away all remnants of those thoughts from my body.

When I've finished I grab the towel from the

radiator and dry myself. When I return to the bedroom I notice something has changed. I search the room for anything different. Has Koen been moving furniture around again? It's then that I see the mirror is missing. A rectangular shape has been left in its place. The cream paint is slightly darker where it had been hung.

I grab the brush from the bedside table and try to run it through without being able to see where it's going. I walk to the wardrobe to fetch some clothes. As I'm sliding a vest top over my chest I notice a folded piece of paper on the top shelf. I slip some clean knickers and some jogging trousers over my legs, pulling them up before sitting on the edge of the bed before to read it.

In the event of danger contact Miss. H. Grayson, 151 Montague Gardens, Reading, Berkshire.

I recognise the handwriting but not the name. When did I write this? And, more importantly why? Was I once in so much danger that I thought I might die?

I decide to ask Koen how it got there. It couldn't have been there long. It wasn't there last night. The only explanation I had for it being there was that Koen had put it there this morning. But why? Where had he found it?

'Alright love?' he says.

I jump.

'Don't sneak up on me like that.'

As I turn around I'm met with someone else. Koen has died his hair light blonde and shaved his light stubble completely off.

He steps forward and smirks.

'Don't you like it?' he says.

My heart skips a beat, then starts thudding heavily in my chest. Before I have the chance to answer him the room begins to sway and everything moves to the right. I no longer feel my legs. My feet to weak to stand, I fall, but I don't feel the carpet as I hit the floor.

I can hear his muffled voice but something else. Someone else over and above him. It takes me a while to understand the jumbled words as they form and repeat, ever more sinister until I catch it. Like grasping in the dark for the light switch. I hear them deep and insidious. Quiet and softly spoken words, above the hoarse gritty sound of Koen.

'Scream quietly or they'll hear. Then you'll have to tell them.'

I'm still frozen in fear but the room is back to how it was before. How it should be. He's watching me now, no longer glaring. He's no longer standing, but crouched down next to me where I sit on the floor. My head in my hands, shaking. But the screaming won't stop.

Terrified wails come from somewhere inside the house. I think at first it's him, but his mouth is closed and he's sitting beside me, holding my hands, trying to bring them down, away from my face.

'Look at me Marieke,' he says, his voice a soft echo below the high pitched cry.

'I can't.'

'Yes you can. Look at me. Everything is alright. Trust me,' he says.

'I can't.'

146

The screaming has stopped. The last sound of it disappeared as I opened my mouth to speak. I want to but I can't. I want to see his face. Feel his arms around me, holding me, keeping me safe but I can't. I can't look at him and I don't want him to touch me.

'Marieke. Do you want me to call the doctor? Is it happening again?' he says.

'Is what happening again?'

'The depression,' he says.

'Im not depressed.'

I'm worried about you. If it's as bad as last time you might need to go somewhere,' he says.

'You want to stick me in a nuthouse?'

'That's not what I said. I just mean that if it's that bad I'd rather you were looked after properly this time,' he says.

'You mean you can't cope with me.'

'I mean I'm not the right person to help you,' he says, standing up and running his hands over his hair.

'I'll lose my job. Is that what you want?'

'Maybe you should take a rest from it all for a few weeks at least, until you sort this all out,' he says, waiting for me to respond.

I jump up and look him in the eyes.

'I'm not depressed, and I don't need help. I just need you to believe me.'

'I know what you went through. You've told me a dozen times how it made you feel. But, it's not getting any easier is it? Perhaps the work that you do is bringing it all back,' he says.

'I love my job. It's the one thing that makes me feel as though I'm doing something useful. Without it, all this has been for nothing.'

'So me and Kate are nothing,' he says, turning around to leave the room.

'Don't walk out and don't talk to me as though you know what's best for me, cause you don't.'

'I'm off to work. I'll see you later,' he says, walking from the room and slamming the front door behind him as he leaves.

I've got four hours before I have to collect Kate from school. Plenty of time to call the solicitor.

I hurry to the wardrobe and slip my hand beneath the folded pairs of jeans. It's gone. I was sure I'd left it there, between the black and grey trouses. It's not there.

I spend the rest of the day searching the house. I can remember the address. Montague street or something, in Reading. I run down the stairs to grab the laptop and slip, landing awkwardly on my foot. I feel my ankle pull and pain shoots up my leg. I stumble into the living room and find it on the shelf below a pile of DVD's and letters.

It needs charging. I plug it into the wall and leave it while I make some sandwiches to eat. I'm not hungry but I need the energy.

By the time the amber light flashes green on the front of the laptop my ankle is swollen and I can't bear down on my foot long enough to stand and walk over to it. I shuffle along the sofa until I reach it and pull it down onto my lap, almost dropping it in the process.

I hear a car turn into the drive and hesitate for a moment. It can't be him. He's not due home for hours.

I lift the screen and it springs into life. I type in

the password and search the address. Just as the details of the solicitors appear on the screen I hear his key turn in the lock and he walks into the living room as I close the laptop and loose the page I was on.

It's a good job I have a photographic memory even if it does cause me vivid flashbacks; the telephone number is imprinted in my head.

'What you doing hun?' he says.

'Just looking up a client's history.'

'I thought we agreed you should take some time off,' he says.

'I think you're right. Which is why I'm considering referring some of my clients on until I feel up to returning to work.'

'He seems pleased with this and comes to sit next to me on the sofa, bringing his arm around me and resting a hand on my shoulder.

'So what are you going to do?' he says.

'I'm going to continue therapy and see how I feel. One day at a time, as they say.'

'Good, I'm glad. Shall I get us something to eat?' he says.

'I've just eaten.'

He heads into the kitchen and returns a few minutes later with a piece of paper in his hand, folded up.

'Where did this come from?' he says.

'What is it?'

He opens it up and passes it to me once he's read it.

'You remember don't you?' he says, after a while.

'I've no idea what you're talking about.'

He passes me the piece of paper and I read the address as if for the first time.

'Who is it?'

'Don' tell me you can't remember. I see it in your face every time I touch you. When we're alone. When I cut my hair. That's not me. I didn't do this to you. You did this to yourself,' he says, throwing the piece of paper on the floor and storming out of the room.

'Koen. I don't understand. I've no idea who that woman is or why I wrote that. I'm confused as shit about all this.'

'All what? What do you mean?' he says.

I realise I have to tell him then, of my lack of memory concerning Alice's father and being unable to remember our wedding. Wondering why there are no baby pictures of Alice and not being able to find our marriage certificate.

'I'm just so confused.'

'I know. That's why I think you should make an appointment with your doctor. See if he has any idea's on what you can do. I'm not qualified to tell you what you need but I know you can't go on like this. For all of us, you need help,' he says, holding me close.

That familiar rotting feeling spreads through my limbs.

'Shit, what happened to your foot?' he says.

I look down. My toes look like they're on fire. My foot is triple the size it should be and has gone purple.

'I tripped coming down the stairs.'

'I think you've broken your foot. Can you hop on one leg? We're going to the hospital,' he says.

He doesn't give me time to reply before he holds me up with one arm and half walks, half carries me out the front door to the car.

There's a light breeze brushing my hair across my face. I stumble and fall onto the car seat just as he opens the door.

We drive in silence for five minutes before he speaks.

'Didn't you notice, that you were in pain I mean? How could you not know you'd broken your foot?' he says.

'I can't feel much. I sat down. When you came in I-'

'You're not looking after yourself properly. It's one of the signs isn't it?' he says.

'I don't know. I can't remember.'

When we get to the hospital he leaves me in the car, returning a few minutes later with a wheelchair. It's only as he wheels me in through the double doors that I feel the panic rise up and flood my chest. Tightening it so that I can only breathe small amounts of air into my lungs. I feel dizzy. By the time my name is called out from the reception area of A&E I can't feel the pain in my ankle any more. My entire body has gone numb.

In a daze I'm x-rayed, my ankle lifted and pressed. A mask of gas is placed over my face. I feel as though I'm suffocating and drifting into a dream-like, drug-fuelled existence at the same time.

When Koen leaves the room to fetch himself a polystyrene cup of hot weak tea a nurse enters carrying a folder of paperwork.

'The doctors going to get you bandaged up. It's not broken, luckily but you won't be able to bear down on it for some weeks. Just keep it elevated and you'll soon be on the mend.

Her blonde hair is cut into a bob to meet her face. She has the greenest eyes I've ever seen. Her face drops and her voice alters a little as she continues.

'I can see in your notes that you've had quite a series of accidents in the past. Breaks and falls and such. Have you ever been tested for bone disorders or balance problems?' she says.

'I was in an abusive relationship before I met my daughters father. My husband is worried about me, but I'm fine. I just slipped and fell. That's all.'

This seems to appease her, and she turns to walk back out of the door. Before she does she stops and asks me how old my daughter is.

'Six.'

'What star sign is she?' she says.

'I couldn't tell you.'

'What's her birth date?' she says.

That's when I wish I hadn't spoken.

'I've no idea.'

'Do you have memory problems?' she says.

'Sometimes. But that's because of the drugs.'

Her eyebrows raise a little then.

'Look I'm a qualified therapist. I don't do drugs. But I had a problem years ago. It's over now.'

That's made her eyebrows raise even more.

'I know how this sounds, but it wasn't my fault.'

I can see any sympathy she may have had for me drain away at this and so I look away as she fills in a form and turns around to leave the room.

She returns a while later with a syringe and a glass vial.

'I need to take your blood. Do you mind? It will only be a small sting and then you won't feel anything,' she says.

'I don't like needles.'

I almost laugh myself at this but she holds it together long enough to pierce my skin and draw the blood up through the syringe. Collecting the dark red liquid in the glass vial.

'What's it for?'

'Just routine. We can only give you painkillers if we are sure there's nothing else in your system,' she says.

'Why would there be? The only drugs I take are contraceptive pills.'

'Like I said, it's just routine. The doctors are very tight on this and I don't want to discharge you without enough pain relief. You almost broke your ankle and the pain might get worse once you're foot is bandaged. I want to make sure I give you the right dose or you'll be very uncomfortable for a few days,' she says.

I lay back on the bed waiting for Koen to return. When he does he looks pale and he can't meet my eyes.

'I hate hospitals.'

'Yeh they're full of pain, illness and death,' he says. 'When can we leave?'

They're waiting for my blood results.'

'What for?' he asks.

'She wants to make sure she gives me the right dose of pain relief or something. Have they got any magazines in the waiting room?'

'I'll see what I can find,' he says, hurrying from the room.

Was it me or were his hands trembling, just a little? Why is he nervous? It's me who hates these places. They remind me of the day I was brought in. The police. The questions. The worried glances and whispered words. The lies I had to tell for them to let me leave.

I shake my head to rid the thoughts but they continue to creep up on me for the rest of the afternoon.

When the nurse returns she takes a seat beside my bed and lowers her gaze as if considering the words she wants to use before speaking them.

'I want you to do something for me. Go to the toilet in the hall and use one of the circle stickers if you need to, okay,' she says, a worried expression on her face, although she is trying to hide it.

She eases me into the wheelchair just as Koen appears at the door, carrying a rolled-up magazine.

He turns his head questioningly to the side.

'I'm going to the toilet. Won't be long.'

He sits down on the chair beside the bed. As the nurse pushes me through the door and out into the hall I notice his foot tapping away on the floor. An anxious expression on his face.

The nurse wheels me into the disabled toilet and waits for me to lock the door. Just as I lift myself up and land onto the seat I hear someone on the other side. Two small wooden doors built into the wall.

'I'm on the other side. When you've left me a sample just pop it on the shelf in front of the little doors and when you leave the toilet I'll bring it through. Remember what I said about the little stickers,' she says.

It's then that I notice the sign in front of me. On the back of the toilet door is a notice asking if you're a victim of domestic violence to place a coloured sticker on the side of the sample pot before you leave it.

'I'm not in any trouble. My husband isn't a wife beater.'

She doesn't reply.

I leave my sample on the shelf as requested without a sticker.

Why would she think he was violent?

When I open the door she says nothing as she pushes the wheelchair down the corridor and instead of heading back to my room we go through another set of doors into a well-lit room.

'Marieke. I need you to be honest with me. It's for your own safety and your daughters that we know the truth. Do you understand?' she says.

'Of course. I know all about safeguarding policies but you don't need to be wasting time on me. There's nothing going on. I'm not a victim of anything.

A knock on the door reminds me that we're not alone. This is a hospital, and she's needed by others.

'Doctor Gillingham gave me these,' an older nurse with fiery red and black hair enters the room, passing the nurse a piece of paper and leaves as abruptly as she arrived.

She reads the words slowly. Re-reading them before folding the paper in half and looking me square in the eye.

'This drug problem. What was it that you used?'

she says.

'I'm an alcoholic. I've been in AA for years. I was in a relationship with this bloke and he introduced me to drugs. I took speed and heroin. It was my choice and my choice when I stopped.'

'But you haven't, have you? I can't give you anything for the pain. I'm sorry,' she says.

'No wait a minute. I'm clean. I have a daughter and a husband. A career helping people. You really think I'd mess that up for one more hit?'

'Your blood test results show moderate levels of GHB in your system. When was the last time you used it?' she says.

I look at her stunned for a few moments before I answer her.

'I've never used it. Isn't it a date rape drug?'

'When was the last time you used drugs?' she says.

'About ten years ago. Why do you think I would have something still in my system now?'

'You must have taken it in the last twenty-four hours for such high levels to be in your blood-stream. It's either that or you've been taking small doses regularly for so long that you're topping it up to a moderate level. Either way you have it in your blood and you must know how it got there,' she says.

'This is madness. I've no idea where you got it from but that can't be my results. I demand a re-test.'

'Okay. I'll take another test. But if it proves true are you going to tell me how long this has been going on for?' she says.

'I don't know. How can I?'

She leaves the room with my second sample and I sit here shaking. What if the test comes back positive again? What if she thinks I'm a drug addict. Will she believe me that I've no fucking idea how that test came back with those results?

When she returns it's to say that my leg can be bandaged now there's a bed available on the non-surgical ward of orthopedics. She wheels me through to a room where a tall thin doctor and his assistant wait for me.

I feel the cool white powdered liquid on my leg as each separate bandage is delicately woven and twisted across my ankle until it holds in place. I still can't feel much.

I'm wheeled back into my room and find Koen sitting in the seat, as though he hasn't moved for the two hours since I was wheeled off. His eyes staring blindly past me then returning to the floor where his foot remains tapping as I lift myself up with my crutches, waiting for him to stand and offer me his hand home.

'Remember what I said Marieke,' says the nurse as we leave the room and head down the corridor towards the exit.

I remember what she said. I can't think of anything else. The words swim into focus and drift past me again and again as I land on the passenger seat of the car and Koen drives us home. As he parks the car up onto the drive and opens the door to help me stand, leading me inside the house with his hand on my back. As he locks the door and runs his hands over his head in relief or exasperation, I don't know.

She said that if I didn't take the drugs willingly,

and I had no idea how they got into my system then someone must have given them to me without me knowing. Without me being aware. Someone must have slipped the liquid into something for me to drink. She said it tasted like salt. She told me to be aware of what I drank and ate from now on. She said someone must have drugged me. Though she couldn't tell me why.

A faint memory flooded my thoughts for a few moments before scuttling back into the deep, dark, recesses of my brain.

The man with light blonde hair and bright blue eyes. The man who seemed to be everywhere. In my thoughts, my dreams, my memories, on the street, in the present. He was here. In this room. I could feel him. I couldn't see him, smell him, or hear him, but I could feel his presence. The energy he gave off. It was hate and venom. Dark and mysterious. Terrifying and real. He was here, in this room. If only I knew where.

'Would you like a cup of tea love?' he says.

'Yes please. I haven't had a thing to eat or drink for hours.'

I sip from the mug slowly. Tasting the sugar and milk. Feeling the warmth it brings to my chest. Lightening it up, freeing my lungs. I can breathe easier now. My chest felt so tight in that hospital. Now I can breathe and stretch and the anxiety has lifted, leaving in place a protective glow. I feel safe and calm.

I finish my drink and place the mug onto the edge of the coffee table, feeling my head grow heavy and my eyes close.

'That's it babe. Just have a sleep. You need a

rest,' he says, stroking my head, running his fingers through my hair.

When I open my eyes I hardly recognise the room. It looks as though a tornado has hit. There's a pile of books in one corner on the floor and a radio in the other, turned down, dull and thumping. An old dance track I recognise from many years ago.

The carpet is covered with boxes and clothes. The coffee table, cluttered and covered in used glasses and plates. Cutlery that's fallen on the floor.

I hear his heavy footsteps before I see him. Thudding slowly across the mushroom coloured carpet.

'You awake?' he says. 'Here have some tea. Just made it fresh.'

I find my hand is too limp to lift and so he places the cup beneath my lips and lifts it up enough for me to take a few gulps.

'That flu must be pretty bad hun?' he says.

I don't feel ill. My limbs are numb and my head is heavy. A little woozy perhaps but not ill. Not fluey anyway.

I gulp back the last of the tea. Luke warm and sweet. When I get to the bottom of the cup I can taste a hint of something salty and not quite as sweet as the rest of it has been but by then my eyes refuse to stay open and the ground swings beneath me. I let my head drop back onto the sofa and listen to his breathing.

'Where's Alice?'

'Over a friends. Thought I should stay at home and look after you for a few days while she's out. Gives us time to spend on our own,' he says.

'Not much fun if you've got to look after me.'

'I wouldn't worry about that. You won't be like this forever. I'll be back to work soon and...,well you won't need me any more,' he says.

It wasn't what he said. It was how he said it. There was something in his voice that sounded as though he'd let something go. A pretence he'd been holding on to.

It wasn't until I felt the darkness swamp me and my limbs grow heavy and tingle that I realised. It was his accent. The tone of his voice had lowered. He spoke in long drawn-out breaths. A whisper. Like someone I used to know. Someone I remembered. It was the man with the T-shirt and jeans. The black boots. It was him. It was Rowan.

JULY 2002

It's hot, and the air is thick. There's no escaping it. It makes no difference whether you're outside or indoors, you can't breathe, you can't eat and you can't sleep. I spend the day slowly cleaning and tidying away the house, having left work early to spend the rest of the day with Rowan. Only he's not here- again.

There's a note on the kitchen work-top.

Gone down South. Back late. See you later. R. x

He won't be back until Sunday. He'll come in with Stevie, a wad of cash and smiles that beam like a shot of sunlight from their wide faces.

I wonder who he's selling those bottles to. I walk over to the fridge and open it to take another look at them and find they've gone.

I can picture his face now. Sitting at the wheel of a camper-van, going ninety miles an hour down the M5. Travelling the length of the country to sell it somewhere else. I imagine some scruffy old man and his wife being stopped by the police a few miles away from where they bought it. Their shocked faces when they find out it's been stolen.

I sip my tea and keep the volume on the TV down low just in case he does return tonight.

By night-fall the house is cold. The darkness almost touching me. I listen to the ticking of the lock on the mantle-piece above the electric fire and realise how late it is when I look up.

I tread the stairs and stand in front of the bathroom deciding where to sleep. Heading to the bedroom at the front of the house. I have to go into the back bedroom to collect my pyjama's even if I don't undress in there.

As I step inside my skin begins crawling again. Like spiders running across my skin. My neck tingles. I feel eyes in the dark, watching me. He still hasn't replaced the light-bulb.

He likes this room. He says it's airy and inviting. I tell him the street-lights from the lane and birds keep me awake. Sometimes we sleep in the front bedroom. But he says it's too cold.

There's something about the Fleur-de-Lys wallpaper that sets me on edge. When I look up from the covers, pulled tightly over my face, so that only my eyes are visible, and see the blue pattern against the white paper; orange in the glow of the street lamp just beyond the window, I feel a knot form in my stomach.

Ever since that morning, last month, when I awoke to find I'd been attacked I can't go into that room. I still don't remember who it was or why.

Rowan made me promise not to think of it. Said he didn't want to talk about it. It must have been someone he knew. Someone who he owed money to. He went off in a rage and came back relieved. Whoever it was he'd sorted them out.

Even though I know he's not here I can hear him. I can feel his presence, smell his aftershave. His voice a constant echo in the rooms, in my head. His spirit follows me. He's always there, in the shadows, in the corners of the room, watching me. I used to think it was Rowan but now I'm not so sure. Since the attack I think it's him. Whoever the person was that did this to me, made me fear my own bedroom, was definitely a man. No woman would have had the strength to leave me with such bruises.

I head into the back bedroom and close the door. Even as I undress I listen out for the sound of tyres on gravel, his footsteps on the path. The squeak of the car door and the heavy thudding of his footsteps as he walks up the stairs towards the bedroom.

I wake up cold. I run my hand down my arm and turn to see that the covers have been pulled off me in the night. He sleeps beside me. His breath warm on the top of my head. His arm reaching out, even as he sleeps, to hold my hand. Though I must have pulled it away in the night.

I creep towards the wardrobe and pull my dressing-gown from the door. I tread carefully from the room and down the stairs, into the kitchen.

As I wait for the kettle to boil I spoon coffee

and sugar into the cup. I pour the water from the kettle as I open the fridge with the other hand. As I grab the milk a bottle falls from the shelf.

I throw it back inside and take a gulp of the coffee, hot and bitter.

I layer a thin spread of butter and a thick lump of apricot jam onto toast, my other hand wiping the window sill. I settle down at the dining table just as I hear him walk from the bed to the bathroom. The shower water a few moments later, splashing the sides of the bath, because I forgot to put the curtain back around it after I cleaned the tiles yesterday.

I hurry from the table and pour Rowan a cup of coffee. Adding two drops of milk and two sugars. I prepare a couple of slices of toast for him, settling them on the table, beside my own breakfast, now cold, and return to the kitchen to make his packed lunch for work.

By the time I've finished he's seated at the table. A cigarette in one hand and a slice of toast in the other.

'The coffee's too weak,' he says.

'You could always make it yourself.'

I stop and shudder at my own thoughtless comment.

'Come here,' he says, his eyes darkening as I step closer.

He stands up from his seat and brings his hand up to my face. Stroking the skin of my cheek, he smiles.

'Make me another coffee,' he says.

I step back and as I turn towards the kitchen he draws his arm back and back-hands me across the face. I fall to the floor as though the breath has been knocked from me.

He leans over me, holding out his hand for me to take.

'Get up,' he says.

I take his hand and allow him to pull me up from the floor. I stand and walk into the kitchen. My hands shaking as I open the lid of the box and drop a tea-bag into his cup. I stand beside the kettle feeling the heat rise from my burning cheek. I find myself pressing my palm against the side of the kettle as the water boils, wondering why I can't feel the heat.

I put his CD on. The rock anthem he likes. It isn't until I call out his name asking if he'd like a drink of vodka form the bottle I bought earlier that I remember he isn't here.

I look down at the latest dress he bought me. The jade one. The one that matches my earings, necklace and bracelet. He bought those too, he bought everything I wear. I like them. They're expensive, feminine, pretty. He likes me to look pretty. Only I know that I'll be back into my hipster jeans, black belly top with the white cross on, the dog collar wrapped across my throat and my nose ring back in place before I step foot outside of the front door.

The speakers vibrate from the electric guitar and the thudding of the floor from the drum-beat reminds me to turn it down. The next track reminds me of my friends.

I haven't seen them for ages. I haven't called

them for months. I miss them but Rowan doesn't like it when I mention them. I try to make the most of the time I get to spend with his friends. Jacky, Sophie, Karen and Donna. But it's not the same. They're all older than me. They've known Rowan for years, though not as well as I do.

They're friendly enough but I notice how they look at me. with wide eyed expressions as if waiting for something. As though I'm about to impart some secret. I can see in their eyes both what they want me to see and what they're trying so desperately to hide. I see it all. The eyes truly are the windows to a persons soul. I wonder what colour my soul is? Is Rowans darker?

The closer we get to the door of the pub the more he watches me. He follows my gaze to see where my eyes drift, to see where they look. I decide to keep my eyes on the ground. It's safer that way, he can't accuse me. I won't meet the gaze of another person, another man.

Throughout the carvery he continues to watch me. It's an unspoken rule that I must not break. I must smile and nod and answer him politely. I can only look to his friend when I'm asked a question or my opinion is required.

He nods in approval at my answers. I must be pleasing him. I loosen up, only lightly. I don't want to say the wrong thing. I must still censor my words. But my second vodka and coke since the first at home is making me feel lighter. I can breathe easier. By the end of the meal he seems looser in himself too. No longer do his eyes wander in my direction so often, but when he does meet my eyes they are bright blue, sparkling. Filled with admiration and affection.

On our way back to the car he seems pleased, happy even. He smiles at me, his eyes no longer searching, questioning my every word; he knows I've passed the test. I only wish I knew what the exam meant.

It seems I'm to find out when we get back to the house. He has a present for me. A reward for my good behaviour. A bottle of champagne and a box of Belgium chocolates.

'These are for you,' he says. 'I want us to celebrate.'

'Celebrate what?'

'Our engagement. I want you to marry me,' he says.

He kneels down on one knee, brings a small silver grey box from his pocket and hands it to me. I take it from him and open the lid. The little hinge snaps and the diamond set on gold between two sapphire stones glints back at me. He takes it from the box and places it onto my finger. I don't need to say yes. He knows I will. He knows I'd never want to be with another man. He knows I'd never look at another. He knows I'd never want to feel another mans skin against mine. He knows I love him.

'What do you think?' he says.

'It's beautiful.'

'Just like you,' he says.

He seems pleased with himself. Pleased that I allow him to put it onto my finger without holding back. Pleased of my approval for his choice of ring.

Pleased for having chosen the right time to ask. Well he didn't exactly ask. He said he wanted me, he wanted my commitment, he wanted me to be his wife.

I've waited so long for this moment that I feel nothing but happiness for him. Happy that he got it right; the time, the ring, everything is perfect.

As I watch him draw the curtains to black out the lamplight from the window and walk over to the bed, pulling the covers away for just a moment, allowing the cool night air to layer my skin with goosebumps before slipping in beside me, I feel something shift. I know without knowing that something wonderful is going to happen. Something magical and special is being released, something has grown between us; an unspoken promise, an unsaid agreement. I've made a promise to be with him always, through everything, no matter what.

Rowan is making a vow to love and protect me forever, to remain loyal and to keep me safe, just like he said he would. Just as he promised that day at the party, when he said, 'I want you to be my girlfriend. I'll treat you right and I'll look after you.'

That was twelve months ago now, but he kept his promise. He had treated me well, he did look after me and he always told me how pretty I looked. He did make me happy. I'm just not sure he still does.

As I nestle my head against his chest, with my back to his stomach., his legs encasing mine, his arm wrapped across my own, I think of this. I think back to the many happy memories we've shared so far and I look forward to more.

I allow him to lift his hand and stroke my hair,

folding it behind my ear. I let him pull me over onto my back and climb on top of me. I let him raise my hands up above my head and hold them there, in his own, his fingers entwined between mine. I give myself to him. Allowing him to control the pace, to decide when I will feel that rush of pleasure take me over, again and again.

Afterwards I let him take his fingers out from between mine and hold me there a few moments, his heavy hands on my wrists, his thumbs pressing down into the palms of my hands, his face close to mine. His eyes piercing mine, watching. Holding my gaze a second longer than I feel comfortable with. His muscled body pressed against me, his chest against mine, heavy and hard, so that I can feel his heart racing, thudding against my own.

'Look at me,' he says.

I didn't notice that my eyes were tracing his skin until he spoke.

'Look at me,' he says.

I raise my eyes as he tilts his head back so that our eyes meet. His are glazed over, as though he's not quite there, his mind somewhere else. I can't hold his gaze. His eyes have darkened, the blue has dimmed. In the light of the small lamp on the bedside table and the moon they are black.

'Look at me,' he says, his voice now a hard whisper.

He's two feet above me. Leaning over me. His weight balanced only on his hands, pressing down heavy, onto my wrists.

I look into his eyes once more. He brings himself closer, moves his face forward until his eyes are only two inches from mine. I'm transfixed by the steely glass look he has over me, holding me there with his mind.

'You're a dirty little whore,' he says.

I'm speechless. My body grows tense, rigid to his touch. I suck the air from the space between us and hold it in but I can't breathe it back out.

He continues to draw in and back out again, his body inside mine, his breath on my neck. The scent drifts from his skin to my nose, Lynx and whiskey.

He brings himself to orgasm and as he reaches the point of ecstasy I moan. I low pitched wail, But it's not from pleasure. His grip is so tight that the bones of my wrists feel as though they'll snap. It's a moan of pain. A sound I've heard many times before, but I can't think where or when.

I listen to the wind blowing the leaves of a nearby tree. I hear the distant knocking of a woodpecker scrambling in the dark. The rumble of a car passing the street. Echoes of voices far away, words of cheer and drunkenness. I see the moonlight grow bright from behind the curtains, casting a shadow over the wall. I follow the shadow to the Wallpaper set in orange, though I know it's white, from the street-lamp outside. The blue Fleur-de-Lys pattern etching itself into my memory. I follow the crest of the half-circle as it leafs off to meet with a triangular shape, like a cross shaped lily. My favourite flower no more.

I turn my head away. I don't want to see the shapes on the wall. I don't want to see his eyes any more. Cold and hard, dangerous. Not exciting as I once found them, but cruel and frightening.

I twist my head away as he folds his arm across me, holding me close to him. I can feel his dampness against my back, his groin pressing against me.

He falls into a deep sleep as I keep my eyes on the curtain, watching the darkness turn light. Listening to the occasional rumble of a travelling car pass the street turn to dozens as the night becomes morning, the present becomes past, the life we once shared become a distant memory. One which I'm unable now to ascertain exactly when or how it changed.

I know it wasn't this night. I know it's been altering, turning and twisting for a while. I just didn't know until this day, this moment, that it had already happened. I didn't know until now that I'd become a woman trapped in an abusive relationship, when just hours before I'd been a girl with a loving boyfriend.

I feel the bed dip and rise, his weight pressed against me no more. He pulls his arm away from me and looks down at where I lay. I feel his eyes on the back of my head. He walks across the room and out of the door. I listen to his footsteps as he walks down the stairs.

It was Joe who told him. I should have known. I should have been more careful. I should never have agreed to go over there. He'd called while I was out at Lee and Amanda's. He told Rowan I wasn't at his. He made me swear I wouldn't go out without him again. I promised myself I wouldn't. I didn't want to make him angry.

I think about what he said, wondering if I've imagined it. He looked me in the eyes as he spoke.

171

He didn't look as if he was lying.

My hand is still shaking. So much that I almost drop the mug of coffee, spilling it down my chin as I bring it up to my lips.

'You imagined it. You always have had a vivid imagination. You can't deny that,' He says.

I know I didn't imagine it, dream it, invent it or in any other way make it up. I'd woken up to the sound of heavy breathing. He was on top of me. I could feel nothing. My body numb from the alcohol and shock. I just stared in the darkness. His whiskey breath on my neck. His hands clawing at me like a ravage animal. I closed my eyes when I caught his and turned my face away so that I wouldn't smell him. I knew what he was doing but I couldn't register that it was happening to me. When I opened them again I wasn't in that room any more. The one with the Fleur-De-Lys wallpaper. I was standing on a bridge. There was a tall man with dark hair stood beside me.

'Everything's alright, you're safe now,' he says.

That's how I learnt how to leave my body. Float up onto the ceiling looking down on myself. Was I dead? I could hear my breathing below his. I could see my body clench and tighten, trying to burrow myself inside the mattress. My chest rising and falling. I was still breathing. I was alive. But I was also standing above myself, on the top right hand corner of the ceiling looking down. Watching.

I closed my eyes and sank into a dream-like daze, knowing that my eyes were still open. I watched him leave the room and drifted into sleep, my eyes close.

A sound downstairs makes me jolt awake. My

172

mouth is dry and my limbs move heavily as I stand and make my way towards the bedroom door.

That's when he enters the room.

'Go back to bed. I've got you a drink,' he says.

I sit on the edge of the bed and sip the hot coffee, spilling it down my chin.

'Last night. You hurt me.'

'Are you having nightmares again?' he says.

'No.'

'Why don't you stay in bed. You look like you need some more sleep. I'll call work,' he says. 'I'll tell them I won't be in.'

He asked me to give up my job last week. He said he had enough money to take care of us both and that I'd get to see him more. But I can't. I enjoy my job. Chatting to people all day, coffee in one hand, cigarette in the other. Though I agreed to take a few days off, so we could spend some time together. I'll spend today, as I spend every day, in his house waiting for him to return from work.

'No. It's fine. I'm fine. Go. I'll be okay.'

'I've got a fight tonight. Some of the lads from work will be there. Will you come?' he says.

'Okay.'

He rarely asks me if I want to do anything any more. I know he wants me to say yes, so I do. It's easier that way.

I stumble from the bed and walk towards the wardrobe to dress.

'Wear the grey top that ties up at the end with some hipsters. They've got the air conditioning on in there and you might get cold,' he says.

I take it from the wardrobe and lay it on the

173

bed ready for tonight. Then I grab a dress from the hangers and slip it on over me. He smiles, leaves a kiss on my cheek and heads out the door to work.

I don't argue with him any more. I just do what he asks me and bite my lip if I feel a comment or that anger rise up through my chest, threatening to spill out. I know if I don't keep it under check I'll do something stupid, and it'd be me that pays the price.

I hang around the kitchen all morning. Scrubbing the floor and wiping down the worktop. Cleaning cupboards and sorting through the cutlery drawers. I find a knife. A small, thin one, used for chopping tomatoes. I slide it into my pocket and take it upstairs. I slip it between the pillow and pillow case on my side of the bed and pray he doesn't find it before I have to use it.

All the while I do these things I think how abnormal it would look to someone else. Why does she stay? When will she walk away/fight back/ go to the police? I used to think these things too until I found myself in this situation.

If I leave he'll kill me. If I stay I will defend myself. I'm not a grass and know better than to go to the old bill. Besides what will I tell them? I live with a man who has more friends and family than I do. He has VIP entry to most nightclubs. He's a boxer, trained in self-discipline. He's a well respected worker and member of the community. He did a charity fight, where proceedes went to Women's Aid. Who is going to believe a girl who says she has been beaten up by him every day since they met but who chooses to stay with him despite this fact? I wouldn't believe her, would you?

Later I hear the engine of the car start and the gravel on the driveway crunch beneath the wheels as he pulls off and drives away, to where and to whom I don't know, but I have an idea and it's not something I wish to think on for too long.

I don't move until the sound of the engine disappears and a few minutes have passed. When I do I feel the sickness rising up from my stomach. I get up from the bed and run to the bathroom to throw up.

I want to rid this low ache in the pit of my being. I want to get it out of me. I want to see it spin and disappear as I flush the toilet. I know I feel as though something has happened. Something irregular has broken the spell of our existence together. But I can't quite put my finger on the very thing. The one thing that slammed the rocking boat down and allowed the water to start filling in. Am I drowning myself or is he holding me down?

JULY 2015

As I come round I notice that the house is quiet. The familiar sounds of laughter or toys being thrown against one another from Alice's bedroom have gone. The constant low hum of the fridge in the kitchen has disappeared. There isn't a sound in the house apart from my own heart beating slowly and lightly against my chest. As if it isn't that interested in keeping up its steady rhythm any more.

Something isn't right. The house is empty. Where is Koen? And more importantly where is Alice? I can't remember the last time I saw her or heard her, or him for that matter. Was it yesterday or the day before?

I look down and see that I'm still wearing the same clothes I wore to the hospital but my ankle has been freed of its bandages. Have I been to the hospital already to have them cut off? Did I do it myself? By the state of my fumbling hands I doubt it. Somebody must have done it for me.

I stand and almost fall back down again as a wave of nausea floods me and I woozily drag myself up and walk toward the kitchen. I need a drink but I can only manage to tilt my head below the tap and allow a small trickle of cold water brush against my lips and onto my tongue.

My thoughts are jumbled and my head still dizzy as I try to think back to the last thing I remember. It's no use. It's like I've been asleep for years. Like Sleeping beauty. Didn't she take a bite of a poisoned apple? I shudder at the thought.

It's as I make my way up the stairs and glance around the bedroom as I enter it that I remember the piece of paper I was looking for. Before Koen returned, and I closed the laptop. Before he insisted on driving me to the hospital. Before we returned, and he made me a cup of tea.

That was it. That was the last thing I remember. He kept passing me cups of tea. I was getting sick of the stuff. One of them tasted funny. Like that doctor said. Like salt. That's it isn't it? I'm being drugged. I've been left here on the sofa, in the house for so long that my ankle has healed.

Did he cut the bandages off me? Has he been drugging my drinks? How long has this been going on? Where is he now? He might be back at any moment and then I'll have to curl up on the sofa and accept another drink from him, pretending that I don't know what's going on. Pretending that I don't know what he's been doing. What about Alice? Where is she? Is she in danger? What was that telephone number? I have to think. I have to remember. I have to get out of here.

I find my walking is slow and struggled. That's the drugs. If I can walk then I must have been laying here, in these clothes for weeks. How did I go to the toilet?

I hurry up the stairs and grab a bag. I throw jumpers, tops, a bra, some knickers and a pair of shoes into the bag. I run down the stairs without fastening it, just as I hear a car pull up outside the house. He's back. I recognise the sound of the engine.

I run to the back of the house and find the spare bedroom is locked. Why is it locked? It's never locked. I run into Alice's bedroom and close the door just as the front door opens.

I hear him walk into the living room and back out. He's standing at the bottom of the stairs, hovering, waiting for a noise. I mustn't make a sound. I stay still for a few moments before I hear the shuffle of his feet as he slowly makes his way up the stairs, calling out my name.

'Marieke, where are you? Are you upstairs?' he says.

I decide now is the time to hide and so I wait for each step he makes before I slowly and carefully slide myself beneath Alices bed. A row of cuddly toys sit on the floor at one end and I fight the urge to grab them and stuff them under the bed with me, hoping that if he takes a quick look, all he'll see are several fluffy animals packed tightly beneath the bed. But he'll know where they'd been, wouldn't he? He's been the only one in the house for hours, perhaps even days, besides me and he would know they'd been moved.

'Marieke. Are you here?' he says.

He reaches the top step just as I make one last quick movement and fold my legs up behind me so that I'm curled into a ball below the bed. My head resting on one arm so that I can still my breath as he enters the bedroom.

His boots are right in front of me on the left of the bed. I can hear his movements hurried but controlled as he looks around the room. He's still standing at the side of the bed. I fight the urge to sneeze from the heavy set dust surrounding me. I place my hand over my mouth and try not to swallow.

What will he do if he finds me? He can't be mad at me. I've done nothing wrong. Why am I even hiding? I should just confront him. Ask him why he did it. After all these years. After everything I went through with my ex, the lies, the violence, the drugs, why would he do something like this? Why would he drug me? How long has it been going on?

'Well if you want to talk, I'll be downstairs,' he says, walking back towards the door and making his way down the stairs. One step at a time, hoping he'll catch me out and I'll move as soon as he hits the bottom step.

I won't. I'll stay here all night if I have to. I won't let him know I'm here. I want him to think I've gone, that I've left the house and gone to seek help.

It's as I'm considering when it would be safe for me to leave the bedroom that I hear the front door opening and closing. The lock in the door. Had he locked it when he last left? Is that how he knew I must still be in the house? Is he waiting for me outside the front door? Hoping he'll catch me as I try to leave?

I remain where I am for what feels like hours before I hear my stomach groan and my leg begin to twitch. My arm, where my head has been rested against it, heavy, begins to grow numb and my elbow aches. I stay a few minutes longer until I know I can't hold it any longer. I sneeze quietly in my hand as I drag myself out from beneath the bed and stand weary, waiting for another sound.

He must still be at the front of the house. I haven't heard the car engine yet. He can't have left. He hardly walks anywhere these days.

An image flashes through my mind then. A woman hiding beneath a bed. Cowering from the sound of footsteps as they edge closer to the bedroom. The door handle coming down and the door almost knocked off its hinges as he enters the room. I freeze, in fear and shock. I can hear flames spitting and smell the faint scent of burning. He's angry. I can see his face and one shoulder in the mirror as he passes it. A heart tattoo with a thick scar running down through the middle of it.

I can hear him too. His voice calm and steady.

'You've done it now. First you stab me, then you try and burn me in my sleep. I knew you'd try to kill me. I knew it wouldn't be long before you did it again. Now you're going to pay,' he says.

Just then I jump and smack my head on the cabinet. I try to find my way half-blinded to the doorway and to the top of the stairs. It takes me a few seconds to realise there's someone standing at the bottom, leaning against the front door. Keys in his hand, swaying from side to side. A smile on his face; knowing and gleeful.

AUGUST 2002

I don't move yet. But I know that when I do I have to move fast and I want to have the plan already set in my mind before I do.

When I can trust that he won't be returning, that he's not forgotten anything, I jump from the bed and run to the wardrobe. I clamber into my jeans and a T-shirt. Sink my feet into my wedge heeled pumps.

My head is clear and bright. For the first time in ages I feel sober and alive. I'm wide awake and bear the energy of a superhuman. I grab a bag from below the clothes rack and begin to throw clothes in as fast as I can. As I pull the zip tight to close it I notice the blue thumb prints burnt into my skin.

The bruises are evidence that this time I haven't dreamt it. Evidence that what happened last night wasn't just a figment of my imagination, a fantasy, a hidden desire that I've projected onto him. I'm not going mad, crazy or otherwise delusional.

All those times he told me that I had no commitment to reality, that I was insane, that I dreamed things and made them real in my head, that I was a liar and that my elaborate tales would never be believed; it was all lies, he was the liar, not me.

I go to fetch the jewellery from the dressing table and stop when I pick up a solid gold necklace, the chain dangling between my fingers. It's not mine, none of it is. It's his. He bought it all. He owns it. Even the clothes are not mine. I drop the bag on the floor and make my way down the stairs as quickly as I can. I want to be out of here now.

I don't look back as I open the front door, slam it shut and run. By the time I reach the end of the road I've cleared my mind of all thoughts, except one. I've managed to focus my mind for the first time in so long that it feels almost forced. As though the thoughts are those of someone else, another person has taken me over. Whoever it is is determined and has the energy of a child.

My one thought is to escape. To leave and to never look back. I know it's my choice, the first decision I've made in the last twelve months and it both frightens and excites me. I'm curious to know what it will be like. How I'll manage without him. But, at the same time I'm scared of what he might do when he realises I'm gone, that I'm not coming back. What will he do? Will he be mad with me? Will he try to find me or will he let me go? Will he even care that I'm gone, or will he get on with his life as though I've never been a part of it? Will he find someone else? Will he love her as he has loved me? Will he miss me? Will he try to win me back? What will I do if he does?

There's nothing I can do now. It's too late. It's too late to change my mind, too late to run back, too late to ask for his forgiveness. I have to keep running now, no matter what, I can never stop.

I don't want to get the police involved but I have nowhere else to go. I have nowhere safe to disappear to, so I use a telephone box three miles away to call them. I tell them I want the number for a refuge. They give me the number but I only have a few notes on me. I leave the telephone box and walk into the nearest shop for some change. I find myself back in the telephone box with a small bottle of wine. I gulp it back as I dial.

The woman who answers tells me I need ID and have to get myself to Highfield. I have no documents with me and by the time I leave the telephone box I've drunk the entire bottle and promised to get there as soon as I can. I know I'll be turned away when I arrive without any evidence of who I am or where I've come from but I decide to make the trip anyway. What choice do I have?

The entire journey from the street where I call her, onto the bus and up to the doors of the house that she told me to go to has taken less than forty five minutes, but I've spent the entire time looking over my shoulder. My body trembling with anticipation and anxiety even as I'm greeted at the door and shown into a side room at the front of the house, next to the kitchen.

I stand and wait until the woman who introduces herself as Pam chooses where to sit, before I seat myself on the chair nearest the window.

A short woman with mousey brown hair pops her head through the partly open door.

'Would you like a cup of tea or coffee?' she says.

'No, thank you.'

'Marieke, did you manage to get any documentation?' Pam says.

'No. I'm sorry. I couldn't go back.'

'No worries. Just fill this form in. It won't take long, then we'll get you settled in. This will help us to get copies sent over for benefits or housing costs,' she says.

I hadn't thought of that. I take the forms and a pen from the desk beside me and fill it in as neatly as I can.

'Nice hand-writing,' she says.

It's the first compliment I've had in a long time and I find myself smiling. This perfect stranger shows me only kindness and sympathy and not the disappointment and frustration I had expected.

'You don't need to tell me why or how you got here, only know that we are here for you and that you are safe now. Wherever you've come from you will find this a safe place where routine and humour keep us together and make us whole again. There is one requirement while you are here. As long as you stay here you must not tell any person where you are and men are not allowed in this building at all, under any circumstances. Aside from that you can do as you please,' she says.

'Thank you.'

I don't know what else to say or how else to express my gratitude to this woman who has offered me so much in such little time. I'm in awe of her.

She shows me up the stairs and takes a key from her pocket, offering it to me.

'This is the only room that's free. It was only vacated this morning and has just been cleaned. I can see you haven't been able to bring anything so I'll get Rhona to drop some towels, toothpaste and a hairbrush in for you later. Don't worry about food or clothes we can sort that out. Dinners at five o'clock so have a rest and we'll see you downstairs later,' she says.

'Thank you Pam. That's very kind of you.'

She stops at the stairs.

'That's my job lovey. There's a phone in your room should you need me for anything. I'm only downstairs,' she says and descends the stairs.

I open the door and flick the switch on. The room glows. I notice the thick brown curtians and the mauve and green patterned duvet. The red carpet and the cream walls. Nothing matches, nothing fits, but it's mine. My sanctuary, my safe haven, my refuge, my home, until I can figure out what to do next.

I lay my head on the pillow and try to adjust my body to the springy mattress and the molded pillows which I expect have been slept on many times by many women.

I watch the cloudless sky become tainted with chunks of cotton. The impending rain sitting above the no longer sunlit streets below. The sky is grey and dull, lifeless and thick. The world has been stained with a weather which matches my mood.

I flip over onto my front and let my arms fall over the sides of the single bed, breathe in the dusty air, listen to the child who cries at the end of the hall for hours, wanting her father, until at last her mother comes stomping out of a room, picks her up and carries her downstairs.

A few minutes later I hear more doors open and close in varied degrees of distress. Footsteps sink, slide or bound down the stairs. I force myself up and out of the door to join them.

A few minutes later we're sat together around a large corn coloured table. Hinges latched together below to hold the thing up. It's flimsy as I pull my arms up from my lap and with elbows on the table, tuck into the food presented to me on a chipped plate.

Chicken, carrots and potatoes slide down my mouth as women chirp to each other, ignore one another or attempt to keep their child from stabbing their fork into an other's food.

I eat as quickly and silently as I can, wondering where the bathroom is, looking around the table at this dysfunctional bunch of people. A family thrown together through fear and violence.

One of the women has a deep purple bruise covering one half of her face. Her lip is curved in at one end. Her wrist is bandaged. She walks with a limp to the sink and washes her own plate before scrambling off and out of the room. A loud angry woman warns her son to stop kicking the table before she jumps up in fright as the door to the kitchen opens and Pam enters to look for a cup for her coffee. A gentle ferret looking woman tries to force her meal down, with a concentrated look on her face. Her eyes examine each morsel twenty times before she places the food into her mouth and chews it for hours. A child is banging and slamming a truck on the floor, then against the wall, roaring like a lion as he does so. A woman with scraggly hair and a blouse that will not remain buttoned over her vest repeatedly does the buttons up between leaning forward to eat and has to continue the process again and again, as each time she leans forwards the blouse falls open once more. The woman beside her drops a large dollop of gravy onto her jeans and begins laughing. I drop my fork and it sloshes a pile of carrots onto my lap. I look around for something to use to wipe it off with and find the loud woman has stopped talking and is staring right at me. She smiles, then laughs. The woman with the gravy on her lap looks down at the mess she's made then laughs too. I can't help myself but join in and soon we're all in hysterics. The entire table sharing an unspoken joke. A secret. That we're idiots. We're useless and can't even eat without making a mess in yet we managed to find ourselves here, together, an unintended family of women who can't seem to be able to look after themselves.

The loud woman pats me on the shoulder as she leaves the room. The others bumble about, tears rolling down their faces from laughing too much. Two of the women go to the sink to wash up. I follow the others up the stairs and we each walk to our separate rooms, alone, without speaking.

When I open the door to mine I find the lamp in the corner on top of the bedside table has been left on. A pile of towels, a new hairbrush, toothbrush, toothpaste and a set of clothes are laid out on the end of the bed. A packet of biscuits, a kettle and some tea bags sit on a tray with some UHT milk cartons and a small white cup, a teaspoon propped up inside it sits on the dressing table. A small black TV has been left beside it. The ariel, a coat-hanger jutting out of the back.

I'm both pleased and saddened by this. Pleased that Pam cares so much for me, has thought of everything, and, saddened that it's come to this. Saddened that I've left a house filled with expensive and beautiful clothes, jewellery, food, drink, a large TV, hairdryer and smart shoes for this; a half-empty room the size of a shoe box containing only a selection of second-hand gifts, charity.

I'm walking from the refuge to the little shop in the corner when I see him. I've no idea how he found me, where he got the address. Had I slipped up, written something down?

He crosses the road, his face beaming. He comes right up to me as if everything is alright. He seems to be forgetting the fact that I've left him.

'I miss you baby girl,' he says, placing his arms around me and lifting me up from the floor to plant a kiss on my forehead.

'So you're living round here then. Not a very nice neighbourhood. Why don't you come back with me. Stay at mine if you like?' he says.

'Rowan, I don't want to come back. I want to stay here. I live here now.'

'Sure, that's great. So let's hang out,' he says, smiling.

'I don't want to. We're over.'

'What do you mean? You don't want to be with me any more? Why? Haven't I treated you right? Bought you everything a woman could want? Taken you out? Is that not good enough for you? Am I not good enough?' he says.

I want to say 'no, you're not,' but I can't, something holds me back.

I see the loud woman round the corner and walk up to the front door of the refuge. I don't want to draw his attention to the place so I ignore her. But she doesn't get it, she doesn't see what's really going on here and walks right over to us.

'Hi, I'm Marieke's friend,' she says, holding out her hand to him.

'I'm Rowan Marieke's fiance. So she lives with you then?' he says.

She hesitates a moment then he follows her eyes to the refuge.

'Actually no. I live here. Marieke lives around the corner. We say hello and share a cupa sometimes. I've gotta go. It's good to meet you,' she says, winking to him or me I can't be sure.

'She seems nice,' he says.

'Yes she is. Look I don't know what you're doing here or what you want but I'd like you to leave.'

'Oh I'm not going anywhere baby. Not without you. I'll stay all day if I have to. Sleep in the car across the road. I'm not leaving here without you by my side,' he says.

'How did you know where I was?'

'I knew you'd be someplace like this. You always like to play the victim. I thought I'd find you staying in one of these places with helpless battered women. Is that what you think you are. Cause you're not you know?' he says, smiling a forced smile that doesn't quite reach his eyes.

'I'm here because I don't feel safe around you. Because of what you did, and that makes me...'

I look down at the ground unable to quite believe the words that are about to leave my lips.

'That makes you what?' he says.

'You've hurt me Rowan.'

He considers this before stepping closer and taking my chin in his hand, looking me in the eye.

'I would never hurt you. I love you. You know that. Now stop being silly and let's go home and sort this out,' he says.

'I don't want to go to your home. I don't want to sort anything out. And I'm not a silly, stupid little girl-'

'Fine. I didn't want to have to do this but you won't listen and I can't reason with you if you don't listen so I'm just going to have to...'

He lifts me from the ground before I can think to scream. Joanne is long gone now. The street is empty except for an elderly couple who keep their gaze to the floor as they walk hand-in-hand, not talking to each other and ignoring my protests.

He flings me into the car and slams the door, smiling to the couple as they walk past. I hear him say 'gotta practice carrying the bride over the threshold for our wedding.'

The man looks up, meets my eye and smiles,

nods to Rowan and continues walking. All the time I thump and kick, pummeling the door and kicking the window. He's put the child-locks on the car. I can't get out.

He opens the driver's door but slams it shut and locks the car on the inside as I try to grab the door from his hand by leaning over the seats.

'You're not going anywhere. You can kick and scream all you like but I'm taking you home where you belong,' he says.

'I don't belong anywhere and definitely not with you. When I get out this car I'm going to-'

'What are you going to do? Call the police? Find a refuge? And tell them what? That you willingly left a refuge to return home to your fiance. No-one will believe a fucking word you say now you stupid bitch,' he says, turning the key in the ignition and driving off.

The wheels screech as he skids and swerves out of the way of an oncoming truck. The driver beeps. I yell at him through the window to 'help.' I kick and punch the door and look back at the empty road behind us hoping that someone will drive up close to the car at any moment and I'll be able to show them, tell them that I'm being kidnapped. But nothing comes, no cars, no people.

By the time I see traffic and realise it's my chance to plead for help we're on the motorway, going ninety miles an hour.

He turns the radio on, switches the volume up and opens the window on his side. Even if someone saw us now they wouldn't think it was strange that a woman was in the back of a car zooming down the M67 with the music blaring.

Perhaps no-one will believe me now. Pam might have seen us talking from the office window. She might have thought we were getting back together, that I'd planned it, this meeting. She might think that I wanted to leave. After-all he only carried me to the car once we'd passed the refuge. All they would have seen was him carrying me over to the car after I stood there for several minutes talking to him.

Why do you only think of the things you could or should have done or said afterwards? After an event has happened. When you're in the situation you can't think clearly.

I watch the signs shoot past and disappear in the distance. We're heading south. I've worn myself out and my knuckles hurt from hitting out at the door and window. I don't seem strong enough to break anything but myself. I decide it's better to save my energy. Maybe I should calm myself and act compliant, then as soon as he opens the door I'll have the energy to run, as far away from him as possible. I'll run to the nearest person, the nearest shop and tell them. They'll call for help and I'll tell the police if I have to. I'll do whatever it takes to get out of this. I don't trust him.

He pulls into a junction. The car slows. We're in Bristol. The air is smoggy and I can feel the grit filtering through the open window and into my nose, my eyes and hair. He had to put the wipers on twice to clean the windows before we left the M5.

We reach a crossing and turn off onto the bypass. The car speeds off as suddenly as it did when we left and we're once again on the motorway.

I must have fallen asleep, watching the trail of people and traffic, the white lines in the tarmac road, shooting past. My eyes hurt and my mouth is dry. I never did like being a passenger. The car rolls along and down onto a country lane. We're surrounded by trees and the smell of manure. When at last I see a sign that says 'Clovelly' I realise we're in Devon.

He pulls over on the side of a green. The grass is light and fluffy, cut short. The smell of fresh summer air hits me, reminding me of a holiday. Friends laughing and drinking. He holds my hand and we dance beside a roaring fire. Later we tell ghost stories and climb into bed. Then the memory fades and I'm back inside the sweltering car.

There are no people, only animals. There is no traffic. It's quiet and secluded. Too quiet, Too secluded. I sit myself up in the seat, realising that I've not been wearing a seat-belt all this time. We've travelled almost five hundred miles. What if we'd crashed?

I lean my head against the cool glass of the window and wait for him to open the door. When he does I don't know what to say. I can't think. All the words I wanted to scream and throw at him before have melted in the heat. Like dust, they float away every time my mouth opens.

'I know, it's beautiful isn't it?' he says, misunderstanding my inability to talk for awe.

'I want to go home.'

'We will in a few days,' he says. I wanted to show you something first.'

'No I mean I want to go back to my house.

Where I live.'

'You're so ungrateful. I've driven you from one end of the country to the other for a break, which I think you need, and you don't even say thank-you. Get out the car,' he says.

That's what I wanted to do. That's what I've been trying to tell him all along. I was going to run from the car as soon as he opened the door but he's already disorientating me from my own ideas. My plans are disintegrating before my eyes. How does he do this to me? Turn my thoughts to dust as soon as he speaks.

I step out of the car. My legs aching from being seated for so long. There's no-one around. Not a sound in the distance, of a voice or car. I'm trapped.

He slams the door and locks it, takes my hand and grips it so that I can't let go and walks me over to a style where the grass verge meets a corn-field.

'Where are we going?'

'Stop asking so many questions and just enjoy yourself. We're taking a holiday. I'm going to show you what we could have if you'll let me. If you'd stop acting so childish-'

'Childish? I want to go home. I don't want to be here. I don't want to be with you.'

'Then go,' he says, letting go of my hand so that I topple into the ditch.

'You want to go, then fine, leave. Find your own way back. But I warn you it's getting dark in an hour and you've got no money. You can't even call your friends in that house. So you may as well come with me. At least I'll keep you safe,' he says.

I realise he's right. I've got no money. How would I get back?

When we got to the holiday home he wants to snuggle up on the sofa and watch a film. I sit next to him with my arms crossed over my chest. My eyes darting from him to the TV, wondering when he'll start. He doesn't.

The following evening we take a treck through the woods and that's when it all changes.

In the darkness of the swollen branches, the violets and bluebells in packs beneath them, I see it again, the darkness form behind his eyes.

I have a vision of him bludgeoning me to death out in the furrows of the sycamore, then burying me beneath them. No-one would find me. Nobody but he knew I was here.

I swallow hard and decide that we should leave the woods. He doen't want to. He's planned a picnic.

'It's too cool and dim. We should take the picnic stuff out onto the field and eat in the open sun.'

'I like it here. You go and burn yourself if you like but I'm eating in the shade,' he says.

I follow him over to a group of large willow trees, shadowed from the sun, on the damp muddied leaves, where we'll picnic without a blanket.

He spends the rest of the holiday, if that's what is must be called, silent, with only the occasional outburst of affection. He spoke to me only when he wanted sex.

I regret it now. Walking back up to the house. I regret staying. Though I had little choice. I was not able to leave. With no money and no sense of direction, what else could I have done?

I slept beside him. For the first time in almost two years we were happy. But I could feel in the air something rotten, something decaying. I tried to keep my mind clear of all thoughts, convinced he could read me. Convinced he could see inside my mind. I decided not to plan anything while we were away. Instead I played along. A pawn in a game of chess. An opponent. I matched his smile. We were both hiding a film of pretence. He wanted to believe me. I acted convinced of his own lies. We played our parts, and it was easy.

By the third day I knew I no longer loved him. I wanted out. I was going to leave. I had to plan it and continue to act normal. I knew if I left he would kill me, so I had to make sure he could never find me. If I stayed I would die a slower death, more painful and less dignified.

I decided to leave by December. That would give me enough time to give him a sense of my continual devotion to him. He would trust me again and I would be safe in the knowledge that he thought he was still in control.

When we got back to Sheffield I slipped into a routine. I wanted to show him that I couldn't be beaten. That I would always come out fighting and I was sure that I would win. My plans faltered the minute I saw him. The minute I looked up to meet his eyes and felt as though his gaze was baring my soul. The only way I could be free of him was to comply. Act the mouse, let him think I accepted his part, the eagle. I was his prey and he would always catch me. I had to present to him a facade of ignorance. Of immaturity and of willingness. I wanted him to see me as a meek and mild woman who would not leave her future husband for anything, not even to protect herself.

JULY 2015

'I knew it wouldn't take you long,' he says.

I must look confused because he steps forwards and continues.

'You know about the drugs. You know it was me and you want to know why,' he says, sitting on the bottom step.

'Yes.'

'I'll tell you but you must promise you won't leave me. You can't leave me. Do you understand?' he says, looking up at me. A glint in his eye tells me all I need to know.

It isn't his eyes, blue, azure. It isn't his smile, a smirk. It isn't his voice which sounds familiar and yet not at all like the voice I'm used to. It sounds more relaxed. Less forced. It's his choice of words. That's what Rowan said the last time I left.

The day he brought me back after the incident. The day I decided never to try to leave him again. 'You can't leave me,' he'd said, before asking me if

I understood what he meant. I understood. I knew he'd kill me if I left. I understood now too, that's what he meant. Koen or Rowan or whatever he wanted me to call him.

He cups his face in his hands as I take the first step down. He looks up and see's that I'm willing to listen, so he continues.

'When you walked out that last time. After the...incident, you said you wanted out. You left me a letter. It said you were going away and never coming back. I couldn't find you at first. I was scared and angry. I knew you wanted to believe me that's why I kept it up,' he says.

'Kept what up?'

'When I found you, I'd dyed my hair and wore contact lenses. You recognised me straight away but it was as though you'd given up the fight. At last, you'd stopped fighting me. You wanted to believe, I think, that I'd changed, that this change in appearance had altered me. My personality, my attitudes were different. I felt different. I thought as long as you don't piss me off, as long as I take on board what the police said and do that anger management programme we could start again. You and me, together forever. Another chance. You played along. You came home. You willingly came to my bed and when we had Alice everything was fine. But then you changed. Something changed. I didn't want you to think of leaving me. I didn't want you to start hating me. I didn't want to lose you so I decided to let you do whatever you wanted. Be whoever you wanted to be. I wanted you to be so happy with me that you'd never want to leave. That's why I had to do it, he says.

I swallow hard, knowing what this means.

'Alice is yours?'

'Yes,' he says.

'Why? Why did you drug me?'

You knew about the other girl. You knew about everything from my past, because we shared it. That's why I thought if I could keep you subdued, just a little, then you wouldn't care so much about the past, but then you had the crash and started all this therapy yourself and it started messing with your head. It brought it all back. Bit by bit I knew you'd start to wake up. I panicked. I never meant to but I had to. Don't you see that? I had to make sure no-one ever found out,' he says, a single tear falling from his eye.

'What happened with that other girl?'

'What?' he says, shaking his head as though he's forgotten already.

'You said there was a girl. What happened to her?'

'Her old man came around shouting the odds. You let him in. He said he was going to call the police, tell them I was a child abuser and-'

'What do you mean? You never-' Wait. You were messing about with his daughter? She was fifteen.'

'You weren't much older than her yourself you know. That doesn't make me a child...anything,' he says.

I gulp back a sob which threatens to heave up from my chest and rack my brains to think of something to say. Now he's being honest I may as well be too.

'You were a drug dealer.'

'No more. That's in the past. I don't do that shit

201

no more,' he says.

'You were violent.'

'Have I laid a hand on you since?' he says.

'Fortunately for you I've been doped up to the eyeballs and compliant all these years. How many?'

'How many what?' he says.

'How many years has this been going on? How many girls have you-'

We got back together about six months after the incident, so 2003-'

'Twelve years?'

'I guess, yes,' he says.

'The girls. How many of them and what did you do with them? Did they run drugs, what?'

'That girl, Emma, she wanted me. She wanted to be with me. She used the drugs to get at me,' he says.

'You slept with her?'

'Only once-'

'Any more?'

'No. No I never slept with any other girls,' he says.

'Just me then? You didn't think it was strange having an underage girlfriend?'

'You were almost sixteen. Hardly underage, and let's not forget that it was a mutual decision. You wanted to be with me. I never forced you,' he says.

I knew the only way I was going to get out of this was to feign compliance as I had in the past. Keep him on my side. Make him believe I was with him, that I trusted him.

'No. No you didn't. I need to think about this. I need to think about us and about what all this means. I think I should spend the night in a hotel and speak to my counsellor. I need to talk to someone.'

'Oh, I can't let you leave. You said you'd never leave,' he says.

'I'm not leaving. I'm thinking. I'm not taking anything with me but a change of clothes and a hairbrush. I just need to think. I'll be back in the morning.'

'What is there to think about? You love me don't you? We have a child together-'

Something snapped inside me. I could feel the pressure like a tightly woven cord, pressing in on me. My chest was on fire.

'I have no memory of our wedding day, of giving birth or days out. I can't remember the last time we went away on holiday, our daughter growing up, her first steps, passing my driving test, getting clean off drugs. I don't remember anything of my life for the past thirteen years in yet you expect me to be Okay with this. Rowan I need some space-'

'You're not going anywhere,' he says, standing up from the bottom step, just a few feet from where I stand.

'Then I'll have to make you listen. I'm not leaving you. I just need some space,...to think. I'll be back as soon as I've figured this out.'

'No. You don't understand. You're not listening. You're not leaving this house ever again. You're not stepping foot outside of this house. You're going nowhere. You can think all you like but it doesn't change anything, does it?' he says.

'I'm going. You can't stop me.'

SEPTEMBER 2002

I'm lying in the bath. The water filled almost to the brim. Scalding hot and steaming up the shower glass and mirror. I don't want to see my reflection. I don't want to acknowledge her any more. When finally I decide to step out and dry myself I hear the front door slam and the sound of heavy footsteps pounding up the stairs.

I sit on the edge of the bath, dripping water onto the lino, waiting for him to call out for me, then I can decide what kind of mood he's in and alter my own accordingly.

'Marieke, are you home?' he says.

He sounds chirpy. I smile. If he's in a good mood, chances are he won't be too bothered about what I have to tell him. I'm sure he knows, I'm not stupid, that I've guessed already, but I'd better still act a little dumb, just in case.

'I'm in here.'

He springs the door open so suddenly I jump

back in fright, almost falling back into the bath.

'Did I scare you?' he says.

My heart thudding in my chest so fast I forget what he said.

''Did I scare you?' he says, louder this time.

'You were a bit fast, that's all. How was your day?'

'OK. Had a little luck on a game. We're going out. Get your sexiest dress on,' he says.

I nod in agreement. My stomach churns then. He wants to show me off, but he doesn't want anyone to look at his girl. It'll lead to an argument at some point and I can't stop my hands from shaking to even stand let alone walk from the bathroom, into the bedroom and get dressed up.

By half past six I've managed to find a short red dress. Low-cut, but not too revealing. I slip on some black suede heels and grab my leather jacket from the coat hook as he slides his arm behind my waist and walks me to the car.

I notice it's an MR2, not the bright red Escort he drove to work in this morning.

'Where did you get the car?'

'It was cheap,' he says.

'Um yes, but where did you get it?'

'D'ya like it?' he says.

'Yes. It's gorgeous.'

He flashes me a smile as I sit down, and reverses off the drive before I'm able to put my seat-belt on.

'I've been thinking. You should go out more. I've invited Jacky and Donna over Friday. Thought you girls could all go out for a few drinks,' he says.

'Sounds good.'

I try to hold my smile and bite my lip. Why am I going out with your friends mum and your dads girlfriend instead of my own friends? Perhaps he wants to keep an eye on me or set a trap. I won't play along to his game. I'll go out and enjoy myself with his money though.

As we turn the corner and park up outside the pub I see Stevie and Gemma's car. So we're on a double-date then.

Inside the pub is heaving. The heat making me giddy before I've even ordered a double vodka and coke from the bar. His eyes are everywhere, searching. I see Stevie and Gemma sitting on a corner table at the back, beside the jukebox.

'I won't be long. Got something to do. Stay here,' he says.

I walk over to the table opposite where I'd been sitting and before I pull the chair back to sit down his arm is across my waist. His breath on my neck. I let go of the chair and it drops to the floor with a thud.

'I thought I told you to stay there, by the bar, where I can see you. You never do as your told,' he says.

His voice is low. Almost a whisper and I know I'm in trouble but I've no control over my reply. It's as if I've been holding it back for months.

'Don't talk to me like that. I'm not a child. I only moved three bloody feet.'

He looks at me for a few moments and then passes me the keys.

'Get in the car and stay there,' he says.

'I thought-'

'Do as you're told,' he says.

I stomp away with my head held high, not wanting him to think he's won this one. When I get back to the car I sit in the drivers seat wondering if I should just drive off and leave him there. I'd have to keep going though. He'd go mad if I left. If I ever left again I'd never be able to come back.

I don't realise how much I'm shaking until he storms back to the car, leaning down to where I've wound the window down.

'Give me the keys and get out,' he says.

I jump out as fast as I can and get back in, seating myself down in the passengers side this time.

'Don't ever do that again,' he says.

He drives fast through the streets until we get back to his.

'Aren't you dropping me home?'

'Dressed like that, no chance. You're staying here with me, where I can keep an eye on you,' he says.

So we're back to that are we?

The first time he got jealous was the day after I'd left his. Joe walked me down to the bus stop and waited for me to hop on as Rowan was too drunk to stand. That morning he met me with his fist, convinced me and his brother had shared a kiss as we waited for the bus to arrive. His brother hit him back. I was too shocked to consider doing that and so I'd accepted his apology minutes later without thinking about it. After-all he wasn't like that all the time, was he?

Now I know better. I know that as soon as we get home he's going to lose it. I think about prolonging the journey. Pretending I've forgotten my toothbrush, hoping that he'll cool off in the supermarket car-park while I take my time looking around the shop. But then he'll probably accuse me of chatting up strangers in there and he'll be in a worse mood than he is now.

I keep quiet as he parks up on the drive and wait for him to get out the car before I do.

'Get inside you stupid bitch,' he says.

Have I got time to make a run for it? Could I get far away from that house and him? Or should I fight back? I won't be quick enough to run or fast enough to hit him back with enough force to make him stop and think.

'Are you coming or what?' he says.

'Yes. Sorry.'

He holds the front door open for me, then waits for me to pass him and step inside before he closes and locks it behind him.

'Get upstairs,' he says.

'What, why?'

He smirks. A sly smile. A discomforting feeling rises up from my feet and into my chest, sitting there like a brick. The crushing panic comes in waves and I fight the urge to scream and kick.

Fighting makes it worse. He enjoys it. He likes the challenge of a fight. It's better to let him do what he wants. Give him the satisfaction of a tear or cry of pain, it's over quicker then. Besides I can get him back in other ways.

I follow him up the stairs knowing I should have made an excuse or told him there and then That I'm not going to put up with this crap any more, but it's too late now. I follow him into the bedroom. The one at the front of the house. He closes the door and locks it.

'I've called in sick so I won't be expected at work tomorrow. You should too,' he says.

I'm about to ask him why but before I can open my mouth he's knocked me to the floor. I can taste blood instantly. He gets on top of me straddling me, landing another punch on my face. I bring my arms up to shield my face from another blow as I feel his fists against my ribs and arms. He drags me up by my hair and forces me to stand. I watch as he walks over to the wardrobe and takes out his black leather belt. He wraps it in half like a coil and snaps it around my neck. I can feel the pressure against my throat as he strangles me. I hit the ground hard as I fall. Too dizzy to stand. To weak to fight back.

'Just kill me if that's what you want. There's nothing left you can do now, that you haven't already.'

'Oh I'm not going to kill you. Just mess you up a bit,' he says.

He laughs and continues drawing the leather in; tightening and then letting it go just before I loose consciousness.

I clasp my hands around his, trying to tug them away from the belt. When I realise this isn't making it any easier to breath I stick two fingers in between the gap and try to leverage it away from my throat.

Eventually, he stands and releases it. Pulling it away from my neck and throwing it across the room. He sits next to me on the carpet, leering at me. His spit landing on my cheek as he speaks through gritted teeth.

'When I do kill you, it won't be like this,' he says.

He walks away, unlatches the door and leaves the room.

I stand woozily and try not to look into the mirror as I make my way downstairs. In the kitchen he's slicing bread. The long, thick knife glinting like his eyes.

'Sit down at the table. I'll make us something to eat,' he says.

He's a psychopath. When did everything get so shit?

I plaster thick amounts of green eyeshadow beneath purple to give myself an eighties look, and to cover the black eye. Foundation so thick, you'd need a trowel to get it off covers fading bruises and bright purple lipstick covers the healing slit to my lip. I haven't been to work all week but at his request I'm going out with the girls for a few drinks.

As I leave he hands me six twenty pound notes and a small bag of speed.

'Enjoy yourself,' he says.

I think back to this morning. How sick he'd felt after brushing his teeth with his toothbrush and sipping another cup of coffee I'd handed him after he'd thrown the other one back up.

I use his toothbrush to scrub the toilet and have been lacing his morning coffee and evening tea with rat poison all week. He's only feeling a bit under the weather. Perhaps I'll have to up the dose.

'Have a good time,' he says, kissing my forehead, like he used to do all those months ago when he saw me off to work. Now I feel nothing when he kisses me. Just numb and dirty.

'I will.'

I'll enjoy myself. I'll have a good time. I'll get drunk in the pub, then drag them off to a nightclub and flirt with every man I meet. No I won't. I'll sit on the edge of my seat, gazing into the bottom of my glass on the closest table to the bar and listen to Jacky bang on about her new beau and Donna's breast-feeding problems. I'll wish I was somewhere else. I'll feel as though I'm being watched and I'll have to stick with the women in case he calls and wants to speak to one of them. I might get drunk though. It'll lessen the pain of the blows when he picks a fight with me tonight.

I head out the door and into the car. He's driving me there and picking me up. Even if I wanted to make a run for it I wouldn't get the chance. He'll probably sit in the car around the corner of the pub car-park, waiting for me. I've got three hours to enjoy myself and he's expecting me to snort speed and drink. I will but I won't feel the alcohol so what's the point. Or is he hoping I'll be hung-over tomorrow but energetic and confident tonight. What's he got in store for me when I get home?

I can imagine but I'd rather not think about it. Not before I get to the pub. I need to feel the rush of power and strength the speed gives me. I need the gear when I get home to calm me down. Help me swim back inside of myself. I want to feel

211

the inner warmth and caress of it as it threads and weaves itself through my veins, soaking me through with careless and complete serenity.

He knows I can't keep off it. He knows that if I leave him I won't be able to get hold of any and I'd come back for more. Not more of him, but more drugs. It was the drugs I needed, not him. Did he know this? Did he care?

I spent most of the evening listening to the women telling me about their latest holiday or the new watch their husband had bought them. The size of a gun Jacky found in her sons bedroom. The ammunition in his bedside unit when she was clearing it out. The baby's feeding troubles didn't come up once and I was in half a mind to ask how it was all going before the conversation got turned towards when I was thinking of having a child, and would I want a boy or girl, when Rowan came up behind me. Holding the back of the chair and leaning down to plant a kiss on my cheek.

'We'd better be heading off ladies. I can see you've looked after my gorgeous girlfriend and had plenty of fun. Now the parties over. Your carriage awaits babes,' he says, pulling my chair away before I've got the chance to stand up out of it. He's strong enough to drag a chair back with me sitting on it. I must weight less than I thought.

I pass the ketchup to him. Watching as he takes great delight in zig-zagging it across the chips. The smell of vinegar and salt making me want to retch. The sickly sent of Dettol in the air is still wafting up from the table. The blood has gone now. There isn't a trace of it left. No evidence of what had happened only hours before.

He sits smiling to himself as though sharing a private joke with his own thoughts.

So you want to kill me?' he says.

'What?'

'You want me dead,' he says.

'No. Why would you think that?'

'You don't sare me, you know. You're not strong enough to do me any damage so you might as well just give up trying now,' he says.

I wasn't planning on killing him. I only meant to hurt him, like he hurt me. I wanted it to stop. I wanted all of this sorry mess to be over with. I wanted my boyfriend back. I wanted to feel his loving arms around me and not want to fight him off or feel the room begin to spin every time he came close to me. I didn't want to be his punch-bag any more. I didn't want him to be mine either.

'So why d'you do it?' he says.

'I don't know.'

He drops his fork and runs his hand along the cut, congealed blood oozing from his forearm.

'You did a good job. You've ruined my tattoo,' he says, smiling.

He laughs.

'Don't do it again OK, or I'll snap your fucking neck,' he says.

'I won't.'

What else can I say? I aimed for his chest but he moved out of the way. He turned so fast that I sliced the knife through the skin of his arm. Right through the heart where my name sat. At least he didn't have my name etched into his skin any

213

longer. It looked like March, not Marieke. He'd have to get it covered over. With something else. I hope he doesn't plan on having my name written over it, again.

'I'm off to work and then I'm going straight to the gym. I'm expecting someone to come and collect something later. When they call make sure you ask them their name and give them the package in the kitchen,' he says, standing up and leaving the plate of cold, soggy chips on the counter.

I'm in half a mind to look in the bag when he leaves but what would be the point? I know it's drugs. I've guessed that whoever it is has already paid up. I know what drugs they are. The same ones I've been taking myself for the past year. Ever since we met he's been my dealer. Was I his guinea pig? Or his whore? After-all he gave me drugs for free and I fucked him. Did that make me a prostitute? Was he my pimp?

He left the house and as I heard the car pull away and disappear down the road I stood up dragging myself out into the kitchen.

He forgot to tell me his name. It didn't matter. Anyone coming to the door was either looking to buy something or came delivering goods to sell.

I was used to this crap now but the anxiety never got any better. I always wondered how long a dealer could do this for before he got caught. Was there an investigation going on somewhere? Were they waiting for the perfect time to pounce and was I going to be here when they raided the house? Or were his plans so meticulously made that he would always get away with it? Just as he got away with everything else.

I run my hand along the cellotaped package. Well sealed and heavy. Inconspicuous in brown parcel wrapping. Like a present, a gift. Something bought from a catalogue or being given away for a birthday. It was not speed. The speed was wrapped in cling-film and left in the fridge to keep moist. This was heroin. About four ounces. One hundred and twelve grammes. One thousand, one hundred and twenty bags. Eleven thousand, two hundred pounds worth of drugs. Sitting in front of me.

I could take it and run. It wasn't like I couldn't sell some of it myself. Most of it in fact. His contacts were associates of his. They'd tell him. He'd come looking for me. He'd find me and then where would I end up? In a ditch somewhere. No-one would find me. No I couldn't do that. It wasn't worth the risk. And what about the man who'd bought it? Won't he come looking for me, wanting his purchase? I'd owe them both, with my life.

Instead I trace a line across the packaging with my finger and allow the idea to sprinkle away into dust. It was just a thought. A very stupid one.

When eventually the bell does ring and I answer it a small, stocky fellow with deep, wide eyes and a solid mass of muscle behind his shirt stands there. It takes me a few moments to think of what I need to say before I ask him his name.

'Buddy,' he says, smiling.

It must be code for something. I leave him standing at the door while I grab the phone and call Rowan.

'What's the name?'

'Bosco,' he says.

215

'Are you sure?'

'What, are you fucking deaf?' he says.

Buddy steps inside the house and closes the door behind him.

'Shit.'

I put the phone down and wait.

'What do you want?'

'Rowan. Is he here?' he says.

'No. He's expecting someone any minute.'

'I'll wait inside then,' he says, walking into the living room.

He seems to know where he is. He must have been here before. I feel a little relieved that he's no stranger to the house but something still bugs me about the way he speaks. He seems to be choosing his words carefully. As though he's being watched or listened to. Recorded. Shit. What if he's Sid? Our code for CID.

It's too late now. He's already inside the house, sitting on the sofa, expectantly. Waiting for something.

'Look. I don't know who you are or what you came here for but my boyfriend won't be back for a while so-'

'I thought you said he wouldn't be long?' he says.

'He won't but he's been held up. What are you waiting for?'

'Don't worry your pretty little head about it. I'll wait for him,' he says, making himself comfortable. His head resting against the back of the sofa and his legs crossed, up on the coffee table.

'Can I get you a drink?'

'Got any beer?' he says.

I walk into the kitchen and as I grab a beer from the fridge I lift the heavy package up from the kitchen counter and stuff it behind the biscuit tins in the cupboard above the kettle.

When I return to the living room he's watching me. His eyes track my movements. His gaze steady and exposing. As though he can see my thoughts before I word them. It reminds me of the way Rowan has with being able to visualise my next move. He brings his hand down to take the can from me and grabs my wrist as he does.

'You're young aren't you? He likes 'em young doesn't he?' he says.

'I don't know what you mean? I'm not as young as I look.'

'No. What Sixteen? My daughters fifteen. Treat you right does he?' he says.

'Yes well, thankyou.'

'Well you call him up and tell him to get his arse home soon or I'll find a reason to call the police,' he says, his eyes now dark and meaningful.

I take the phone and call him, my fingers hit the buttons so fast I almost dial the wrong number twice.

'What do you want now?' he says, clearing his throat and sniffing.

'It's not him.'

'What do you mean? Who the fuck have you let into my house?' he says.

'He says his name's Buddy and he told me to tell you that if you don't get your arse home he'll call the police.'

'Well you tell him from me to get the fuck out of my house or he'll be leaving in a body bag,' he says, slamming the phone down.

I know he means it. I don't doubt that for one second but there's something honest about this man and I want to know what he meant by Rowan liking them young. I decide to tell him that Rowan will be home soon so I can find out more.

JULY 2015

'Get upstairs,' he says, lowering his voice.

Those words promised to shake me to my very core but I tried desperately to show him that they didn't hurt. I want him to think I'm choosing to stay with him, but I have to find a way to get out of this house.

'Go upstairs. You can think in the bedroom. Tell me when you've decided what you want to do and I'll let you out,' he says.

'Don't be so stupid. I'm not being locked up like some mad woman prisoner in my own home.'

'Why not. That's exactly what you are,' he says, before shoving me up the stairs.

I turn and shove him in the chest but he grabs my arms and twists me around, forcing me forwards. I push back against him as he struggles to keep his balance whilst forcing me up each step. As we reach the landing I see him produce a key from his front pocket and open the locked bedroom at the back of the house.

'You can't be serious?'

'Do I look like I'm joking?' he says, before pushing me inside, turning and leaving the room.

As he goes to close the door I grab the handle and claw out at his arm in an attempt to get him to look at me. If he sees the panic in my eyes he might stop long enough for me to force the door open and shove past him. If I can get down the stairs I can get out.

I dig my nails into his flesh but he swipes my hand away and looks up smiling.

'That was a silly thing to do Marieke,' he says, slamming the door.

I hear the key turn in the lock. Knowing that was my best form of escape I wonder whether I can make it out of the window, but I can see that it's been boarded up from the outside. How long has he been planning this?

Is this what he wanted all along? Did he miss his bad-boy persona that much? Had he been waiting for the day I would figure all this out and try to leave, just so he could lock me away like some Victorian wife who'd reached the depths of insanity and he'd finally had enough and decided that instead of getting help, instead of seeking some bizarre treatment from a well-off psychiatric doctor he would instead, treat me himself.

'You can't keep me in here forever. Someone will come looking for me. Someone will want me. Alice will wonder where I am.'

'Alice isn't here any more,' he says, from the other side of the door.

'What do you mean? What have you done with

my baby?'

'She's not a baby any more. She's a girl and she's in safe hands,' he says.

'What do you mean? Where is she? Who's got her? Who's got my baby?'

'You saw to the fact that she would be better off without you. It was your doing that got her where she is. It was your mess, your mistakes, your choice,' he says.

'What do you mean?'

'She's better off away from you,' he says.

'Why? What have I done?'

'Can't you remember? You hurt your own daughter. You almost killed her in that fucking car. You put her life in danger. I've made sure that she can't come to any harm. She's safe, and that's all you need to know,' he says.

'What about me?'

'What about you?' he says.

'What are you going to do?'

I trace my fingers across the wall as I wait for his reply. I can still feel the faint outline of the Fleur-De-Lys pattern beneath the lime green paint. It's slightly embossed. Not visible, but still can be felt if you run your hand along the wall softly.

I never did like this room. I never did like the silence or the complete darkness which you got at the back of the house.

'Rowan, are you still there?'

'What? I've got to go. I've got work to do you know?' he says.

'There's something I need to know.'

'Go on,' he says, his voice being spat between clenched teeth. I can hear the anger beginning to rise up from him. Was he now just a simmering pot, instead of a boiling one? Or had he, until now, until this day, been able to quash his temper? Control it and deny it's existence?

'That day, when I left, you said there was an incident. What was it? What happened?'

I'd remembered as I walked away from the house. The day I'd spoken to the police, who weren't really there. I still wasn't sure if they were a hallucination or if I'd been speaking to someone else entirely and interpreted the conversation differently.

I wait for his reply.

OCTOBER 2002

I try to raise my arm but it's no good. The pain shoots down the length of it as though it's been gripped in a vice and crushed. One side of my face is swollen. My jaw feels as though it's been stamped on. It feels loose in my face and I can't bring my teeth together to meet inside my mouth.

I have to leverage myself up with my other arm and as I sit I feel a snap, hear the crack. Pain shoots from my ribcage as though it is tearing the skin and at any moment will protrude from my side and spring wide open.

I force myself to stand and make my way across the room, slowly as if at any moment I will collapse and my entire body will crumble and fall to pieces.

I pass the front door without a glance and make my way up the staircase. I find him sitting on the edge of our bed, a towel wrapped around his hand. A few tiny droplets of blood speckled across it. He looks at me, holds my gaze for only a few seconds before bringing his eyes down to the floor.

I continue into the bathroom where I find myself staring into the mirror. A girl looks back at me. Her eye is swollen. Her mouth is gaping wide open. A thick bruise from the black eye trails down to her cheek bone. Her other eye is glazed, the lid around it sunken, the skin beneath it is hollow. Her pale flesh sits tight against the bones. Her nose is a thin line in the middle of her face. As though stuck on and added later, as an extra part, one that was not important. She looks ill. Young, damaged, tainted. Her expression is one of emotionless shock. Perhaps she always looks like that but I don't like it. I don't like her.

I open the cabinet door where that mirror sits in front of. I don't want to look at her any more. Amongst the packets of pills and a couple of sachets of Lemsip, I find two of the bottles I saw in the fridge. I take them both out and read the labels again. Xyrem. Sodium Oxybate written beneath. I know what they are but I don't know how. Gamma Hydroxybutyric Acid. GHB.

I put them back on the shelf and bring out a packet of paracetamol. I swallow two, using the ice cold water from the tap. I find a packet of codeine and swallow two of them too, hoping that they'll take the pain away. I sit on the edge of the bath waiting for them to kick in. Before I leave the bathroom I take another two of each, again using the tap water to swallow them down and leave, making my way down the stairs.

I walk into the kitchen and pour myself a large glass of wine. The bottle has been left behind the bread bin for several days. It tastes stale and bitter, like vinegar and fruit. I swallow back as much of it as I can stand. I feel it sitting beneath my chest like a fluid brick, heavy and sedentary.

I don't know how much time passes but I find myself impatient and can't stand the silence of the house. It's eerie, crushing. My stomach churns and I almost bring the wine back up, having not eaten much for so long my body is no longer used to feeling full. I want to strip myself of this crawling sensation forming along my skin, building and covering me in waves. Like one thousand tiny insects are clambering across my body.

I pour myself another glass of wine, letting the last couple of drops slip from the bottle and into the glass like purple rain. Then I sift through the bread bin, dodge the notes, all twenties, and find what I've been looking for. I don't question myself. I don't think. My hands complete the actions they always have without my brain having to intersect.

Once the pills are lined up on the kitchen worktop I count them one by one as I place them into my mouth, one at a time and swallow. Glugging down a large sip of the vile tasting liquid as I do so.

Eventually I find my head begin to dull. The sunlight streaming through the windows dims as though night is falling. But it's me who is falling. Sinking, being sucked through the floor. I can feel the weight of my bones and my head too heavy to hold up any longer. My eyelids droop. The room is alive with water. That's it. I'm being tossed amongst the waves. Bobbing up and down in a rough deep sea. Then spinning, in a whirlpool. Being thrown around. Swirling and sinking, further and further down. Down into the depths of the sea. Drowning.

I can still hear the noisy silence of the house echoing around me. The swishing in my ears and the blurring of my sight don't take away these sensations.

I don't know for how long I lay there. Unable to move, or think, or speak. Eventually I hear movement above. Hear footsteps descending the stairs. I force my eyes open, wide enough to see.

A shadow flits from behind me on the floor where I lay and passes by my feet. I look up. I see him standing over me, watching. His eyes like a laser shooting right through mine.

I can't move. My limbs still heavy from the pills and wine. I want to but I can't. I want to say something but my jaw is still loose. I grind my teeth trying to find where they should meet. I hear a snap and my jaw stiffens. Rigid and no longer loose I find I can move my lips, albeit painfully. But it is possible. I try to make the words but they come out jointed. Slurred, like the moans of an infant or the babbling of an elderly patient who has suffered a stroke. I sound like a child learning to talk.

He bends down and leans over me, his face close to mine.

'What did you say?' he says.

I can't form the words. They slip through the air, meaningless.

He stands tall, turns and picks up the empty glass. Turning it in his hand as though inspecting it, then placing it back into the exact same spot he found it. He picks up the empty packet of

Dothiepin. Crushes it in his hand, then glares at me.

'How many have you taken?' he says.

I don't notice I've lifted my head until I feel it smack back on to the floor. Head back, eyes drifting, sight blurred. I feel my body tremble. Shake and convulse. I can't stop it. I have no control over my limbs. Everything goes black but I'm aware of the sound of footsteps walking away. The door closes behind me. Nothingness.

I awake later. My lips glued together. My tongue dry against the roof of my mouth. The door opens. He bends down and lifts my head up from the cold lino by my hair, then drops it back. I hear the thud. I feel the hard floor against the back of my head. He leans closer. I can feel the warm breath from his mouth on my face as he speaks.

'Ain't you fucking dead yet?' he says.

Tears prickle my eyes. I want to cry but I've no energy. I want to ask him why but I can't form the words. He stands tall and kicks the top of my head. I can't feel anything any more. I'm numb, dead. He turns and leaves. This time slamming the door behind him.

It's only when I regain some sense of where my limbs are and remember how to move them that I'm consciously aware of rising.

I grip the handle on one of the cupboards and drag myself up. Pulling as hard as I can until I'm crouched down on my knees swaying. I manage to stand and lilt heavily as I walk out of the kitchen. I walk along the hallway, past the living room. He's not there. I open the front door and step out. I don't want to look back. I don't want to remember.

JULY 2015

I sit in the room mulling over what he said. Thinking over every word. He made out that it was just a fight. An argument, no different to anything that had come before. But it wasn't was it? He'd left me for dead.

I'd discharged myself that same day. Lee found me. He said I'd left the pub in a hurry, upset. Rowan was drunk. Drunker than any one of his friends had seen him. He was making a gunshot salute, talking about taking a gun to my head when he got home. His friends laughed but Lee believed him. He raced back to ours a few minutes after Rowan had left. He'd driven home drunk, swerving all over the road.

Lee was too late. He knew something had happened when he got there and found the front door left ajar. Rowan had got there first.

I remember his fist coming towards my face. I remember the second punch, landing on my head and then everything went black.

Lee told me when I woke up in the hospital bed, two days after I'd arrived. He told me what had happened. The state that I'd been left in.

Rowan wasn't there when he found me. He'd run off, still covered in my blood. I was lying face down on the cream carpet. The blood soaking through from a cut to my head, bruises covering my legs. I was half naked. He thought I was dead, but didn't hesitate to call for an ambulance. He knew Rowan had done it. He believed me, even if no-one else did.

I only remembered waking up in that hospital bed. Lee was sitting there in a chair. He told me everything. Even the things I didn't want to hear. The things I didn't want to share with the nurse or the police when they took my statement.

That was another thing that puzzled me. What happened after? If we've been together all these years there must have been a reprieve, a break where he sorted himself out as he says he did. Didn't he say he'd attended anger management? Had he been inside? Surely the police wouldn't have allowed him to get away with what he'd done to me. He must have gone to jail.

I was considering this as I heard the low murmur of an engine as the car pulled up at the front of the house. I knew I didn't have much time. Alice could be anywhere and he obviously didn't realise just what he was doing right now. I try to think quickly. What are my options? What would I have done back then?

I knew what I had to do. It would be risky, but it was worth a chance. And, maybe it was only one chance I had left.

I waited until I heard the front door closing, the lock and chain being applied. His heavy footsteps on the thin carpet of the hallway.

'Can I have something to eat?'

Thinking he couldn't hear me I repeated what I'd said and waited for his response as I looked around the room for something heavy and hard. I found a brass candle holder on the bedside table. A vague recollection of it came into focus. A memory, sharp for a few seconds before disintegrating in front of my eyes, like dust after jumping down onto an old sofa that hasn't been used for years.

I was following the lines of an engraved diamond shaped pattern. Small figures of elephants dancing around the bottom rim as though on a merry-go-round. The smack of something hard against my skull. Realising it was a foot. Blood soaked through the pillow. I had to wash it myself.

I shake my head to rid the image as he unlocks the door. He steps inside and I wait for him to come closer.

'What do you want to-'

I bring the candle holder down onto the side of his head. My arms raised high above me, I bring it down again and again until he falls. He grabs my face as he goes down, bringing me down with him.

I realise that with him above me my only option to get out of this is to kick him in the face. I bring my foot up and kick as hard as I can. I jump and stand up over him, bringing the candle holder down once more.

This time he doesn't fight it. It's as if he's given up. He lets go and allows me to hit him once more. His head falls back onto the carpet, and now it's his turn to bleed. There isn't much blood, but enough. I could carry on but I know the police will ask me why, if it was self defence, did I kill him. I don't want to kill him. I want him to stop. I don't want this to carry on any longer. Not as it did before.

I run from the room and lock the door, just as he did to me and call the police from the car as I drive off. Next I tap in the number I've etched into my mind.

Three rings and a woman answers.

'Uh...hello, my name is Marieke James I found a note to myself. I don't remember writing it but it says to call you if I'm ever in fear of my life. I need to know what you can do to help me.'

'Marieke. You're in danger. Can you get here?' she says.

'Yes. I'll be as fast as I can. He's got my daughter.'

I memorise the address she gives me. Repeating it all the way to the motorway and singing it as a mantra as I head South, towards Reading.

The police must be there by now. They must have found him. I gave them my number just in case they wanted more information but I knew I wouldn't speak to them until I'd spoken to my solicitor. She was my solicitor right? I hadn't actually checked. She hadn't said, but then she was at home. She must have been home.

I pick my mobile up from the seat and dial back. She answers a little slower this time. It's Friday, she must be busy with clients. Like I should be. I should be working now, not travelling the length of the country in search of answers and wondering where my daughter is.

'It's me again, Marieke. I never asked you. Who are you and why did I have your address?'

'Hello again. You contacted me about twelve years ago. You told me to keep hold of some bank details for you. You had a secret savings account that you wanted hidden. You said if your life was ever in danger you would contact me. I was to give you the bank details and advise you on what steps you needed to take if you ever wanted to leave,' she says.

'Did I tell you about Rowan. Did I tell you he hurt me? Did you know I had a daughter. He's got her now. He's taken her somewhere and,...shit!'

I swerve and miss by inches a car over-taking me without indicating.

'Marieke, are you driving? Put the phone down and we'll talk when you get here,' she says.

She ends the call before I receive an answer.

By the time I reach Reading I'm dehydrated, hungry, tired and feeling sick. What if she can't help me? What if I don't have enough money? I don't even think I've got a passport. I've never lived on my own. I want my daughter.

As I park up half on the kerb outside a small terrace house with a plaque on the front I know I'm almost there. I've almost reached the point of no return. I'll have to tell her what I've done. Will she defend me? Is she a criminal lawyer or a civil one?

I knock on the door. I stand there for what feels like minutes, but is probably only seconds before she answers.

'Hello, I'm-'

I step inside before she's had the time to finish her sentence.

'I need your help. He locked me in the bedroom. He said he wouldn't let me out-'

'It's okay. Come on in,' she says, walking me into a sparsely decorated living room which has been converted into a make-shift office.

Stacks of paper in coloured folders sit on the edge of a table at one end. A radiator behind it with stuffed animals perched on top. A dark brown blind half covering the window. She sits behind a desk and waits for me to sit, before handing me a small folder.

'Everything you need is in there. The bank details, your driving licence, marriage certificate and my business card,' she says.

'Isn't there anything else?'

'Like what?' she says.

'Plans; where to go, what to do. Did you know about Alice?'

'I didn't know you had a daughter, no. You gave me this twelve years ago. You were in the post office, on holiday and you were so worried. You'd given the cashier a fright, passing her a piece of paper saying 'help me, call the police.' He was stood behind you. As a solicitor I notice things and knew you were in trouble. The cashier made some excuse for you to stamp something away from him and passed the piece of paper over to a colleague. The security for the shopping mall across the road came over and waited with you for the police. While you stood there I winked and dropped my card into your pocket as I pretended to bump into you. You called me three days later from a telephone box. You made some excuse about a training course and we met at my office in the town. You gave me all this,' she says, motioning to the paperwork, 'and you told me to keep it safe, in case you needed it one day.'

'What am I supposed to do?'

'What do you want to do?' she says.

'How will I get my daughter back? How do I know she's safe?'

'Call the police. Tell them where you are and tell them you have a solicitor,' she says.

'I don't even know your name.'

'Helen Grayson,' she says. And, don't you worry. We'll get her back and you'll be alright. Now shall I make us tea while we wait for the police,' she says.

I nod and pick up the receiver.

'I reported an abduction. I'm safe now and I'm with my solicitor. I had to use self-defence...'

Twenty minutes later the police are knocking on the door, just as I sip my tea and think over what they're going to do. After-all in their eyes I'm just as guilty as him. I've injured him, badly.

Two tall, clean-shaven, men appear in the doorway.

'Marieke James?'

'Yes. Have you found my daughter? Is she safe? Is Rowan OK?'

'We are arresting you on suspicion of attempted murder. You do not have to say anything but it may harm your defence if you do not answer when questioned anything which you may later rely on in court. Anything you do say can and will be used as evidence in a court of law. Do you understand everything I have just said?'

'Yes, but I,...I didn't mean to hurt him. It was self-defence. He locked me in the bedroom and...'

I couldn't hold the tears back any longer. They slid down my face and I felt swamped by them. Suffocating in my own misery.

'I want my daughter safe. I don't want her with that bastard. He's violent and abusive. Please...he shouldn't be around kids. Not my girl. Not my daughter...'

I feel hands pressing down on the back of my head as I'm forced into the van. Seconds later it's speeding down the road. I'm a criminal. I'm a violent criminal. That's all they'll see. That's all they'll hear as I stand in that witness box. No-one will believe me. No-one will see what I've been through for it to come to this. Will I be released on bail? Will I be able to see my daughter? Will they charge me? Will the press get involved and will I appear on every newspaper as some lunatic woman who one day just decided to smash her husbands skull in for no reason?

At least I'm safe now. Away from that vile monster and his sick, evil twisted games. The lies and deceit I've lived with for thirteen years. At least it's over now.

NOVEMBER 2002

I shook with nerves as I packed the bag A small holdall. I left it in a neighbours garden, between the hedge and the bins. I left my alarm clock beneath the pillow so that I could feel it vibrate but the sound was muffled.

He was not here today. Had not returned all night. I called him as soon as I had woke to say good morning, to ask how he was getting on. I wanted him to think I cared, that I missed him, that I was looking forward to his return.

He called back twice while I dressed and wrote the letter telling him why I was leaving. He knew I was up to something, but where he was I had at least three hours to get out of the house before he came back. I didn't worry so much about him coming back early. I'd be gone by then, far away. He wouldn't be able to find me where I was going.

I set the letter down on the telephone stand in the hallway and opened the door, feeling the icy winds blowing down the street. I kept my head up, alert to the sounds. Aware of any changes in my view. A car speeding past, a person walking their dog. It was still early so I hoped at least a few people were up and about in case he did come swerving around the corner or in case I did have to put it off another week.

But the entire time I walked from the house to the town, clambered aboard a bus and settled down in my new surroundings, I kept my head up, eyes alert, ears pricked up.

I paid the landlady and was shown into a small green painted room with a bed and a lamp, stood on a small table in the corner. At twelve pounds a night I could not complain. Though it had no feel of home. No comfort or warmth. It was mine now, and that was all that mattered.

I eat dinner alone. A packet of noodles cooked only from the boiled kettle water. I drink tea and lay back on the mattress imagining I'm somewhere else. But each time I close my eyes I'm sent straight back to that house, to him. Perhaps I should remain awake, keep my thoughts on the present. This is safer. This is a kinder place to live.

Eventually I fall asleep with the blanket pulled up high to cover my face. A knife beneath the pillow. My hand clenched around it, even as I sleep.

There are no sounds to this place, it is eerily quiet. Too quiet. I can hear only my breath over the distant sound of trees blowing gently in the wind.

From my window I can see the cathedral. The

ornate carvings and angelic figurines fastened to the tips of turret shaped stone, yellowing with age. Opposite, on the corner is a large gothic manor house. The gargoyles stare at me through the glass, trying to weaken my spirit. Letting me know that even in another city, where nobody knows me, where I should be safe, I'm still being watched.

I'm not to trust that I won't come to harm, even here, on the outskirts of Cheshire, where most of the houses are contained within gated communities and owned by footballers and fashionista's.

I like to think that they're no different to myself. They still have problems, just as anybody else.

Since coming here I feel as though there is something hanging over me. I can't quite shake off the fear, of the unknown, of him finding me. There is still a chance that he will, one day, come walking around a corner or knocking on my door. After-all he found me in a refuge, I'm not safe anywhere.

I decided to stay here as long as I felt safe. Though truth be told, I knew I wouldn't feel safe, ever again. He would find me. The question was when?

I have to be prepared to fight to my death. I have to be strong and fit, able to defend myself to the bitter end. There is no other option but to win. The only way I will go down now, is if I dragged him with me.

I head in the direction of the library. Secluded and quiet, but public and visible. I have to take my mind off of him. I have to blend in and build some awareness over my being here whilst remaining unknown. It would be difficult, but so long as there were enough people who knew I existed without giving away who I was or where I'd come from it would make it more difficult for him to do anything to me, knowing people cared about me.

I still hadn't been in touch with any of my friends. At first I didn't want them to worry about me, then I thought it would be better once I was settled. Now that I've made this county a home of sorts, it feels wrong to invite them back into my world, now that so much has happened. What if they start to ask questions? What will I tell them? Would they blame me or will they worry for me?

I wanted to be sure that I was safe and that he'd quelled his thirst for blood before I contacted them. There was also the chance that he'd called on them looking for me. If I contacted them and they were lying for me, he'll know. He'll be able to see in their eyes if they're covering for me. I don't want to put them in danger either. It's better that I keep my whereabouts to myself, for the time being at least.

I make myself sit comfortably in the chair and settle down with a book at a table beside the check-point and a young student tapping away at a laptop. I'm visible to all and have a clear view of the door. Will I spend the rest of my life keeping watch? Surveying the streets for a blonde man with black trainers. Making sure the exit is clear in case I have to make a run for it?

At least I'm alive. At least I have my life. There are women not as lucky as me, who never make it. Their lives are taken and they never know anything other than pain, violence and emotional torture. I

239

have my life and I have the chance to make something of it. I can continue looking over my shoulder and worry myself into an early grave or I can find out what this world has to offer me.

Though for now, I'll make do with a good book in the library, before walking back to the B&B and sipping on a warm cup of tea in front of the electric heater with the television turned down low, so that only I can hear the muffled voices above the steady rhythm of my own hearts beat, which quickens any time I hear a noise nearby or feel a change in the temperature.

I'm alert to any and all changes of environment, a persons mannerisms, speech, the weather. It's as though I'm connected to the earth and the people, in yet I feel so small and insignificant beside them.

A small child in a big city. I guess I never had the chance to grow up until now. Spending most of my teenage years with an older man, pretending to be a woman. Living in a bubble, a fantasy where everything is fine so long as he's in a good mood. I know how others feel, think, see the world and understand everything within it but I still don't know how I feel, think or see.

I've learnt the things that are not important for most people and have skipped the things that are. Like how to cook a meal, where to shop for shoes, how to act around people, what to say in situations where I find myself not knowing anyone. These are the things that are second nature to most people, but that I am not accustomed to.

Whereas I can tell you where to hide in the event of an imminent attack, the kinds of things a man will say when he's angry, that nobody else will

240

be able to hear and for how long you can hold your breath whilst being strangled before passing out.

I doubt many people in this world could survive a sudden catastrophe. Could outrun a group of thugs or talk themselves out of being shot by an armed robber- I could, and for that I'm proud, if not a little sad that I do know these things. In yet I have no sense of direction, almost passing out if I find myself lost in a crowd of people. I can't take care of myself any better away from him than I could whilst we were together.

Though of course there is more freedom here in this small little bed-sitting style room than there was in that big house where the air stifled any or all of my thoughts with the heavy pressing weight of dread and fear, anger and hostility, but at least back there I knew what to expect. I know what to dread or fear. I know how to stifle my anger and deal with his hostility. Here I am without a reason to be scared or cry in yet I keep finding myself pounding the pillow or curled up into a ball on the floor sobbing. I feel more vulnerable, exposed on the streets than I did in the confines of that house.

I leave the library after fifteen minutes of staring blankly at the words of a book I once loved but can't seem to think why. I can't concentrate any more. I feel the heat rise up and fill my cheeks.

A man walks past the table and winks at me as he brings a chair over, next to mine. I can smell a hint of aftershave and leather. I can feel my chest tighten and I want to get out of here, now. I can't breathe. I have to get outside in the open space and air before I collapse into a pile of trembling, tearful bones, racking and heaving in the fear of panic.

I jump up just as the man sits himself down beside me and almost run to the door. Opening it as quickly as I can so that I can take a huge gulp of air. Only when I get there I find I can breathe in but not out. Oh my God I'm dying.

I hit the floor before I have the chance to throw my arms up out and into the air. Two passers-by, a woman and who I assume is her boyfriend are speaking to me and when I open my eyes I'm being lifted up from the pavement and they both prop me up with their arms and walk me over to a bench at the edge of the high street.

'Are you alright?' she says.

'Yes. I'm sorry. I'm fine. I couldn't breathe.'

'Are you sure you are alright?' he says.

'Yes. I am now. Thank you. I'll head back home-'

'You fainted, you should keep still a moment and-'

'I'm sorry, I can't. I have to go.'

I leap up as quickly as I fell and pass the woman, who by now is standing back, mouth wide open, shocked by my sudden return to health.

This is when I know I can't hide. I can't run. I have to fight. I have to try. I don't want to be like this any more. I want to believe that love exists. That it is still possible, that one day I will find love. I have hope that one day I'll feel safe enough to trust another man. Until then I'll do everything possible to make myself mentally and physically well so that when he comes, which I know he will, I'll be strong enough to make it a fair fight.

I half run, half drag my feet back to the B&B

and lock the door behind me once I reach my room. There is something appealing about returning home to the safety of your own space, no matter how small, after a fright. At least here I know what relief feels like. Back in Sheffield it was temporary. Here it will last, at least a little longer.

I pick at some left-over pasta salad that I bought earlier this morning before the office workers and shoppers filled the streets. I'm eating better. That's one thing which almost immediately changed once I left him. At least I'm not making myself sick any more and I'm trying to eat more varieties of food.

A knock at the door breaks my silent meal. I walk towards it slowly, hoping that by the time I reach it they will have gone. Whoever it is seems to be in a hurry.

I don't think to check who it is. I don't think to call out and ask what they want. Perhaps I should have done. Perhaps I should have thought more on things. Questioned things. Planned for things that may have happened, but it's too late now.

He stands there. His face blank, unreadable. His eyes bright. Wide and glinting. As though he's in the ring, about to fight.

I stand back and go to slam the door on his face but he stops it with his foot. He walks forwards and pushes right past me, almost knocking me over. The door is left open. He didn't lock it. He hasn't locked me in, like he usually would have done. I have to barge past him to get to the door.

I stamp on his foot and run, out into the hall and down the staircase as fast as I can. By the time I reach the lane he's only a few feet behind me.

He pulls a hammer from the sleeve of his sweatshirt and slams it down hard on my thigh. I fall to the ground as he slams it down once more, harder. Then again and again until my legs are covered in sharp pain. When he's finished he stands back, like a decorator admiring his work.

'Get up,' he says.

I force myself to stand and hold onto the wall for support. He steps forwards so that his face is inches from mine. Brings his hand up to my face, pressing a clenched fist in to my cheek.

'I will never let you go,' he says.

'I'm not coming back. It's over.'

'You'll come back. You always do. You're mine, remember that,' he says, turning and walking away.

I want to collapse, to crumble and sob but I won't give him the satisfaction of thinking that he's won. I won't allow him to think that I'm weak and vulnerable. That's how he wants me to be. That's the girl he wants. As soon as I became a woman, he was no longer interested. He gave up caring. He doesn't even seem to care about keeping it all indoors any more. The violence is no longer a secret if he can attack me out in the daylight of the lane, beside a busy street.

I feel rage and relief over any fear that I would normally have felt. Then later came the panic, when I realised that he'd travelled two hundred miles to do this to me. He'll be back. He'll come looking for me, wherever I moved. He'll never let me go. That is one thing I can be sure of, amongst all the uncertainty.

DECEMBER 2002

I lift my head from the pillow. Feel the blankets move around me, one falling on the floor as I stretch my legs. I Hear the distant echo of a trolly. I try to piece together my last waking moments before I fell into this abysmal sleep. My head is foggy and my thoughts are jumbled. How long have I been here? And, more importantly, where am I?

I remember shouting. Was it me or someone else? There was fear. The kind that makes you feel as though you are about to die. Pain. I felt pain. In my head. Like something had hit it.

I try to think back. Trying to gather the fragments. They're distorted. It's like trying to piece together a jigsaw with half the bits missing.

How long have I been lying here?

The curtains that are drawn around me open. A chubby nurse walks up to the bed. She pulls a clip-board from the bottom of it and with a pen from her pocket begins writing something down.

She looks up and sees that I am awake.

'How are you feeling?' she says.

Groggy, disorientated, lethargic.

'Tired.'

'Can you remember anything?' she says.

I shake my head.

'You've sustained injuries to your head and face. It looks worse than it is but we'd like to keep you in for a day or two. You had quite a nasty,...accident and we want to make sure everything's alright,' she says.

The nurse said it was an accident. That I had a head injury. Though she didn't say how or where.

'What kind of an accident?'

'We were hoping you'd be able to tell us,' she says.

'Us?'

The curtain draws back once more and two police officers walk up to the bed. Why are the police here? A man and a woman. With notepads and worried faces.

'Marieke, do you feel up to answering some of our questions?' says the woman.

They want to take a statement. I cannot remember anything.

'When she's feeling better,' says the nurse.

She's very protective that one. I can see it in her eyes.

'Have you got any family,' says the woman.

'My patient is not able to answer any of your questions today. Please could you return tomorrow,' says the nurse.

'We really want you to get better Marieke but we need to know if you remember anything about the incident. We have to begin investigations. It will help us if you could tell us anything at this stage,' says the man.

'Not today,' says the nurse walking the police officers away from the bed and closing the curtain once more. Blocking them out and drawing a veil between us and them at the same time.

I like her.

'Have you got anyone who can come and see you?' she asks.

I shake my head. I don't want her thinking I'm alone. That I have no-one now, but I don't want her thinking I'm some dumb blonde who can't look after herself either.

'I have family and friends but they don't live close. I'll speak to them later.'

That seems to satisfy her.

'I've got to go and check some x-rays. I won't be long. If you need anything just press this button here,' she says, pulling a wire bell across the bed and leaving it beside my hand.

I wait until she's gone before I lift my head from the pillow as I'd practiced and attempt to haul myself up. I repeat these movements several times until I am sat.

I can see the tall table on wheels that can be brought across me, over the bed so that I don't have to lean across to grab the beaker of water.

There is no movement from behind the curtains. No trolly being wheeled down the ward. It is quiet and still. I lift myself up from the bed and stand. Woozy, but able to move so long as I hold on to the bed rail.

Thinking over the words accident and incident it

seems to suggest something unexpected. Unprecedented. Shocking. Something involving others. Other people. Me and at least one other person. Something that causes a head injury. Hit or knocked against something. I come to the conclusion that it must have been a traffic accident. A collision. Was anybody else hurt? Was I in the car or did it hit me?

I ask these questions and more as I look about for something to wear on my feet. I notice a pair of shoes have been left on the chair in the corner, beside the in-built cupboard unit, where I assume patients are meant to be leaving their possessions, but I find I have none as I open the door and shut it again.

I pick the shoes up from the chair and tie the laces, loosely as though I've forgotten how to do it, after fumbling with them for almost a minute. Then I walk to the curtain and open it up.

It's a quiet ward but I'm not alone. There is another woman with a look of horror etched onto her face laying in a bed opposite mine. I wonder if it is a permanent fixture or if I have some terrible facial disfigurement that I'm not aware of. I certainly cannot feel any pain. In fact I cannot feel anything. My body is numb. The only sign that I'm perhaps not myself is the fact that I'm walking a little off. As I pass the frightened looking woman and another, older lady, asleep in a bed beside the door I notice I'm taking baby steps. Instead of what I assume is my usual stride my legs are shuffling. Feet stepping onto one another. As though I've forgotten how to walk. Or have I been laying in that bed for too long?

When I reach the end of the ward, opening the door and letting it close itself, I find myself beside the nurses station. A nurse has her back to me, her face pressed against the telephone. Her other hand blocking out any sounds from the ward. I continue to walk straight ahead, soon finding myself at a set of double doors. I lift my hand to pull on the handle and an almighty shrill sounds from an alarm somewhere.

The sound causes me to startle. I shrink down into a ball. The blare piercing my head like hundreds of tiny daggers. Then I feel hands on my arms. A voice, firm and authoritative.

'You can't leave. This ward is locked. You are quite safe here Marieke,' she says.

The nurse from earlier is standing behind me. She lets go of my arms. Her pale blue uniform fits snug against her frame. She gently pulls my hand free of the handle and brings my arm down to my side.

'You can't go walking about. You must stay in your bed and rest. I've checked your x-rays and they're fine, but you still need to see the ward sister. She has some questions she'd like to ask you. It might help us to frame things,' she says.

The alarm goes off and the nurse steps back.

'I can't answer any questions. I have to leave. I want to go home.'

'The police want to talk to you before you leave this ward. You can't leave yet. Not until we know that you are safe,' she says.

'What makes you think I won't be safe. It was an accident wasn't it?'

'We can't be sure. You need to go back to bed

and rest. We'll talk more tomorrow. I'm going to get the ward sister to come and speak to you,' she says.

She takes my shoulder and turns me around, gently, to face the ward. She stands behind me. I take in my surroundings. The nurse on the telephone has gone. Two more wards lined side by side are opposite me. My only way out is that door with the alarm.

I turn back around, coming face to face with the nurse.

'I want to leave. I'm going home. I may have had an accident but I'm perfectly capable of looking after myself.'

'You can't leave. Not yet,' she says, trying to stand in front of me.

I don't like her any more. She thinks she knows what is best for me. She thinks she can help me. But she can't. No-one can.

I shove her aside as she reaches for the handle of the door. Why is she trying to stop me from leaving?

She lunges forward and grabs my arm.

'Please will you go back into the ward. You can't leave,' she says.

I pull my arm away and shove the door open. The alarm sounds instantly. Glaring ceiling lights blind me as the door swings open.

I quicken my pace, but find I still cannot run. Though I am running in my head. The alarm is a shrill cry, of pain or of anger I can't be sure. But the sound has alerted people. I hear their footsteps running and searching. For me? Or for a way to stop the alarm? As I come to the end of the corridor I'm met with another set of double doors. These are alarmed too. I can't get away from the sound.

I find myself in another long corridor, only this one has two sets of double doors. One on the left and the other on the right. I run to the end and choose the doors to my left. These are not alarmed. The further away from the sound I get the quicker my pace, until at last I find myself halting beside a lift. I choose the staircase beside it, knowing that anyone chasing me will want to choose the quickest route. I'm better off taking the stairs. I hop and glide down them as fast as I am physically able to and at last, at the bottom, come to a set of double doors marked 'exit.'

I pull the handle hard. Feel the breeze of fresh afternoon air on my face. Cool and refreshing. My head is still heavy but the pain is lessened by knowing that I'm free. I let go of the handle on the door and turn the corner. On a grit path I'm met with two nurses, a doctor and the police woman from earlier at their side.

I'm cornered, trapped. I can see a car park behind them. A wall separating us from a field. Too high to climb. Too perfectly straight and narrow to find anything to hold onto to pull myself up.

We're standing silent for a few moments. I see the doctors face twitch. They're waiting for me to make the first move.

'How did you reach me so quickly? Is there a secret set of stairs you can use to follow me?'

'So you came by the stairs, how very clever of you. I hear you are planning to go home, is that right?' says the doctor.

I don't like his smile. His skin wrinkled and pale like it's been stretched and then let go. I refuse to answer him.

The police woman steps forward.

'Please Marieke. We have to speak to you. We understand that you must rest so why don't you come with us back on to the ward and we can talk there?' she says.

'No,' says the nurse. She's not ready yet.

'We really think that when a witness has woken up they must try to tell us everything they know before they have a chance to think about it. That is when the mind can invent things,' she says.

'Invent things? Are you implying that I'm a liar?'

'No. We just want to get all the facts right. A witness is suggestive until they have given their own story. Their own version of events,' she says.

'My version of events? How can I tell you anything when you won't even tell me why I'm here?'

'It is for your protection that you stay here. Until we can sort everything out,' says the nurse.

'Protection from what?'

'You have been involved in a very serious incident Marieke. You have to understand that nobody at this stage can answer questions for you. You must tell us yourself what happened. This is important,' says the police woman.

'My patient isn't well and needs to rest, so if you don't mind we will be leaving now. You'll have to come back tomorrow to talk to her. That's if she's feeling up to it,' says the nurse.

'I'm not ill.'

'You must calm down Marieke, we are all trying

to help you,' says the nurse.

'Calm down?'

'Yes, Marieke. You are getting yourself into quite a state,' says the nurse.

How does she think I'm going to calm down? Or will she calm me? Is she going to inject me with something? Do they think I'm a mental patient? Am I?

'We'll be back tomorrow morning,' says the police woman. 'We'll go through everything then.'

'What is there to go through? I don't remember how I got here, least of all anything about the accident.'

Was it an accident?

The nurse turns me back to the main doors where the exit sign sits above the frame. The doctor waits for the police woman to turn around and head back to the car park. The nurse who has been standing silently beside the one who now holds my arm in a protective and firm embrace steps forward and passes us both. Holding the door open for us to pass through.

This is my chance. I pull back from the nurse, twisting my arm out from her grip and turn, facing the doctor. The police woman now long gone.

'Marieke, I thought you were going to do as you were told and get back to bed. You need to rest and you heard the police woman. They will be back tomorrow to talk to you,' he says.

I don't like his smile or the way he talks. I don't like his choice of words. As though I'm some little girl. I don't like his hard eyes or his perfect white teeth.

'I'm going home and you can't stop me.'

I barge past the doctor almost knocking him over and run. My legs are stiff and weak from being in bed for so long but once I get the muscles moving I can feel them lightening and accepting the speed I take, until at last I am standing in the car park. The cement beneath my feet is a promise of freedom. The sight of the police woman opening up her car door ahead, a reminder that I am not yet free.

I run towards her. See the car dip as she gets inside. Hear the door slam. Hear the engine turn and spit into life. By the time I reach the space where she was parked it is empty. The car in the distance, turning the corner and disappearing from sight.

I want to cry and scream. I want to call for help, but I don't know why or who from. I decide to follow the car. To run from the car park and chase it out onto the road, but I'm too late.

I'm caught off balance. The nurse is holding me back.

'Marieke, will you please listen to the doctor. He is trying to help you. We all are. Will you come inside?' she asks.

'No.'

I stamp on her foot as I run. The nurse who up until now has not spoken or made any attempt to move now stands in front of me. She does not physically stop me but instead stands so that I have no option but to stay where I am and listen to her.

'Marieke. You have been involved in something bad and we are going to do everything in our power to make it right. But first we need you to go back to the ward. Calm yourself as nurse Walton suggests. Then we can talk. I want to hear your side of the story,' she says.

The nurse does not wait for my reply. Instead she takes a step back, standing beside nurse Walton and the doctor. They surround me. I can't go anywhere. They stand waiting for me to realise this.

'I want to know what happened to me. I want to know why I'm here.'

'Then you had better come with us. We can help you,' says nurse Walton.

Every time I try to leave they bombard me. Surround me. Every time I ask them a question they skirt around it, talking about something else. If I'm to discover anything about this incident I can do so in company, rather than alone. I turn around and walk back to the hospital. I decide for myself that the better option is just to follow them back to the ward. Whatever happened, it can't be that bad. Can it?

DECEMBER 2015

Back in my cell I breathe a sigh of relief that it's all over now. The trial was awful. I had to go over everything from when we first met right up to the attack. Helen stood by me and passed me tissues throughout the trial.

It was the first time I spoke of the engagement party. The night he lead me upstairs, away from our guests. What he'd done and what he'd said. Saying it was to remind me that I was his, that I belonged to him and no-one else.

I had to relive the day of the incident. The day he left me unconscious on the living room carpet for Lee to find.

I had to go over the times I'd woken up knowing I hadn't drunk the night before, feeling woozy and disorientated. I told the court about the bottles of GHB I'd found in the fridge. I told them he'd accused me of imagining things, of going mad.

The defence asked me why I'd stayed. Why I

hadn't left. I told them how he'd found me with his money and drugs, in the B&B and how he'd told me I'd have to work for him to earn the money back. They accused me of prostitution. They accused me of allowing him access to young girls. They accused me of being an accomplice to his drug dealing, of lying and of being of unsound mind. I admitted I'd been driven crazy by him for most of my life. I told them I'd met him when I was young, that I was scared of him and didn't realise the trouble I was in until it was too late.

His barrister said Rowan feared for our daughter. That he'd been forced to take drastic action and leave her with a friend while he'd locked me in the bedroom for my own safety. That I'd gone wild and smashed his head in for no reason.

Only my barrister and Helen questioned how I could have found the strength and sudden rage to carry out such an unprovoked attack, as he was a trained boxer. Helen told the court I'd been coerced into an underage relationship with a highly dangerous criminal. That his past behaviour must be taken into account.

I keep going over those same questions myself. Why hadn't I noticed that I was being drugged? Why hadn't I got out sooner? The truth is I was scared of him. I still am. He made me believe all those lies. He told me I was damaged. That I was hallucinating. I didn't want to think otherwise.

I sip the weak tea as I think over the outcome. I've been given twelve months for Grevious Bodily Harm. Alice is living with a foster carer until I'm released. Rowan has been charged with abduction and false imprisonment. He's being held on remand

and is looking at a four year prison sentence. I may not have my daughter, but we both have our life. We've both been wronged by the man who she thought was her step-father and who I thought was my husband. He turned out to be the monster I thought I'd got away from.

I've been on remand for five months so it looks like, taking that into consideration, I'll be released in seven months time. I'll get to see Alice by summer.

I have a photograph that the social worker took for me, blue-tacked to my cell wall. I'll take it with me wherever I go. Whatever prison they send me to. I'll keep it safe and never let it go. I will never let her go. She's never witnessed the horror that echoed the walls of that house. She won't know what I went through or how she came to be here. I'll keep her safe from harm, just as I've always done.

It was last night, as I sat on the toilet in the dark, waiting for morning to come and the sounds of tormented, guilty souls to fall when they slept, that I heard it. With my foot tapping the cold, cement floor, the sound thudding like boots in my mind. Amongst the aggrieved prisoners to my left, my cell being the last in the row, at the far end, nearest the small window, where the draught came through the bottom of the door-I heard it.

'Scream quietly, or they'll hear. Then you'll have to tell them what I did to you.'

I had a vision. A flashback. I could hear the loud thumping from downstairs. The echoes of laughter and the occasional clanging of drink bottles and glasses being knocked together or re-filled. In the darkness of the dimly lit bedroom at the back of the house, my eyes following the pattern of the Fleur-De-Lys wallpaper, I tried to pull my skirt down to hide the bruises on my legs, which were beginning to form. I passed the mirror on the wall as he walked me out, holding my hand, forcing me to face our guests. My mascara had run down my face. Fresh tears beginning to form in my eyes. I blink them back and drag the black sleeve of my cardigan across my cheeks to rid the ruined make-up.

While our guests drank and laughed and chattered away downstairs I was being abused by my boyfriend.

I looked at the back of his head as he stepped out in front of me, still holding my hand as we walked back down the stairs. I no longer saw him as a bad-boy. A mysterious, temperamental but loving, if not a little possessive man. I saw a weak spirited, coward. A boy who'd never had a father. I saw a violent, sadistic, controlling drug dealer.

I spun the ring around my finger hoping that by loosening it, it would slip off or catch on something and break, like my heart. It never did. Neither my ring nor my heart. I wouldn't let him win. I took a vow that day, that I'd never let him win. Whatever happened from now on I'd be the one who was in control. I'd take whatever shit he dealt me but I would come out fighting until the bitter end.

And I had. Hadn't I?

EPILOGUE

Alice is at school. I drive along the narrow verge which leads to the house. I have to see it one last time. I have to paint a picture in my head; a new one which offers hope. I have to forgive him if I'm to forgive myself. I have to see the house where it all happened and relive each and every moment in detail.

I step out of the car and walk up to the door. I knock three times. I half expect him to be there. But I know he can't be. He's still in prison. It's only as I move to walk back to the car that I see the curtain move slightly from the corner of my eye. He's in the living room, looking out, watching. But he can't hurt me anymore.

I knock again, three times, expecting him to run to the door and pull it open. I visualise him dragging me inside and slamming the door, locking it. Locking me in. But he doesn't. His movements are slower. His eyes are misted over. He stoops now, like an old man. His face buried in his hands, hiding from the light.

The sunlight blazes through the house as I kick the door open and run into the living room. I lunge at him, the knife in my hand. He turns and struggles for a moment, trying to fight me off whilst trying to grab something from the table.

I knew how this moment was going to end. I knew it was his life or mine, and I vowed this time it would be him leaving in an ambulance. He would be the one on lock-down in a secure unit of the local hospital. He'd be the one to be loaded with drugs- in the morgue- where he belongs.

I hear loud breaths coming in gasps. My fingers gripping a table. I look up and am met with two large green eyes. A mop of thick brown hair.

'How do you feel, now that you've beaten him?' she says.

'Better.'

It'll get easier with time. Soon you'll be able to visualise him alive and then you can confront him. When you're ready we will work with the police and you can meet with him for real,' she says.

'Yes. I think I'll be ready soon.'

'I think our session today went well. Perhaps you can practice this at home, though less of the violence from now on. I'd like to see you able to confront him and tell him how you feel, in practice for the real thing,' she says, walking over to the other side of the consulting room.

She returns with my handbag and a smile.

'You're one of the strongest people I've met Marieke. You will get through this,' she says.

I take the bag from her hands and walk over to

the door. I stop a moment to breathe and refocus.

'It's a funny thing the mind. When things get tough it almost closes in on itself, shuts down. That's what you have to consider. That you are slowly opening doors back up. Some may never open fully, perhaps not at all,' she says.

'Will the dissociation get better? I mean, will I ever be normal again?'

'Events such as you've gone through change people. But you shouldn't be scared. Try to accept it as another challenge; one you can get through now you have support,' she says, gathering our coffee mugs from the table and following me out the door.

I wave and continue to the front door. Stepping out onto the pavement I take a deep breath of the clean air and head to the car, thinking over all that she's said over these past months.

Perhaps it is time to acknowledge that some things I may never know; may never remember. I must be okay with that.

I reverse out of the parking space slowly, my eyes darting quickly over the suitcases on the back seats.

Later with Alice beside me sipping lemonade through the straw of her polystyrene cup I hit the motorway heading South to Reading; towards our new home and a new beginning.

WRITING SCREAM QUIETLY

The aim of a psychological thriller is to offer the reader a psychological exploration into the human condition. In this case both the survivor and perpetrator of domestic abuse.

I chose a first-person narrative voice to offer you, the reader, a more intimate glimpse into the life of a survivor of domestic violence. At the same time I didn't want it to become a fictionalised version of a 'misery memoir' and so I decided to add the present day life of Marieke, after her ordeal, as a way to provide a positive focal point to the story. Enabling justice to prevail. I also chose to write in the present tense as I felt that a thriller needs a modern edge.

Writing about such difficult issues requires a particular amount of sensitivity when touching upon subjects such as abuse. Whilst I have attempted to keep the plot as realistic as possible I have had to apply a large element of fiction as case studies and real-life stories from survivors are often quite unbelievable with regard to the amount of abuse survivors can endure and the strength in which they have found to overcome, and often grow from it. Such real-life stories are so harrowing that it would deter a reader away from reading such fictionalised events and so I have had to remove some of the gritty details without deterring from the plot and to ensure that the story unfolding remained as realistic as possible.

Throughout Marieke's story I thought what can possibly be worse than death? Living? Surviving an ordeal so terrifying and painful, so emotionally raw and self-defining, that is often worse than death.

The psychology of the abuser is portrayed in snippets of conversation. Reaching the harrowing and thought provoking finale we see what Marieke and many other women throughout the world have experienced and realised after leaving an abusive relationship which began when they were young. That they were not women at all but children of a much more horrendous crime

Grooming is used by abusers to lure their 'victim' in and subdue them into a state of chaos and disorder. After many weeks, months or sometimes even years of charm and what is termed 'love-bombing,' these women find themselves trapped in a cycle of abuse that doesn't always end when they leave. Once they find themselves wanting to get out they realise the danger they have to put themselves in to enable them to break free.

I wanted to show you from the inside just what it is like to be a survivor of domestic abuse and how such subtle and often mind-altering tactics are used to bring a survivor down into a state of submission. Often wondering if it is better to stay, rather than leave. I also wondered what would be worse than having left an abusive relationship, only to find yourself in another one? Something many women experience. That's where the idea came from to give Marieke one further obstacle to overcome. The fact that she hadn't ever left. But had, instead, chosen to deny her present, whilst equally being stuck in the past.

Many women suffer the effects of Post-Traumatic

Stress Disorder (PTSD) during and often for years after escaping, an abusive relationship. Marieke experiences flashbacks and panic attacks, two of the main symptoms of PTSD.

Dissociative amnesia is a form of psychological distancing, which often results from PTSD. We see how Marieke as a young girl has been shaped into a compliant actress, through months of manipulation and control. Through Marieke's narrative we come to understand her as a mature woman.

When Marieke realises that she has not been in a violent adult relationship but has actually been groomed by an extremely dangerous criminal who possibly suffers from some form of psychopathy, and that she was instead a victim of something much worse, we are immediately thrown into a world in which we saw coming but can't quite believe how we came to be there.

The aim of this book is to spread light on the pressing issue of domestic violence and show another side to this form of abuse. Domestic abuse can happen to anyone at any time, at any age and of any social class, culture, race, religion, sexual orientation, or gender.

I also mention in the epilogue that Marieke, through her recovery has decided to confront Rowan over what he did to her as part of her healing process.

The Forgiveness Project was set up in to assist and support survivors in confronting their abusers and learning to forgive them as well as themselves. Many men and women have used their services, finding the process therapeutic.

You can find out more through their website at: theforgivenessproject.com

What would you do if you were Marieke? Would you have known that something was wrong much earlier? That your life was in danger? Would you know if you had blocked memories from yourself in order to survive? Would you have fought back in the end? Or would you have feared for your life or perhaps not trusted your own memories?

I like psychological thrillers that make you think, and make you question your own responses to what you are confronted with. A good book is one which remains with you even after you've turned the final page and put it safely back on the bookshelf. A good book is one which makes you wonder, what would I do in that situation?

If I got you thinking, asking questions, guessing until the very end and wondering what you would do if you were Marieke then I've done my job.

I hope you enjoyed this book. Look out for my next dark, gritty, disturbing and deeply unsettling thriller *Damaged*, available now from Amazon.

ACKNOWLEDGEMENTS

Firstly I would like to thank my ever-patient husband and children for their support in allowing me the time to sit and write for hours without too many disruptions. Secondly I would like to say a huge thank-you to the authors and members of YouWriteOn who have provided me with their comments. Thirdly I would like to thank Hayley Van-de-burgt for her useful medical expertise and knowledge. I would also like to thank my beta readers who have taken the time to review and critique this book whilst it was a work in progress. Namely: Ashton Gilman-Goodlad and Jessica Louise Burtenshaw. Finally to my many readers on GoodReads who were able to provide me with some useful idea's on keeping the theme from becoming too dark. At last I must thank all of my readers, old and new. For without you there would be no reason to write at all.

Louise Mullins is the Amazon best selling author of *Scream Quietly,* her debut Psychological Crime Thriller.

Louise is a qualified Psychological Therapist and writer, currently training to become a Clinical Forensic Psychologist. She lives in Bristol with her husband and three children.

DAMAGED

Even though I've seen the newspapers, read the headlines and watched the television reports, it still doesn't feel real. I still can't quite believe he's so damaged.

A serial killer is terrorising Berkshire.
Everyone is hiding something.
Kira: 'I could kill that man.'
Nathan: 'Some secrets can destroy you.'
Jonathan: 'I'm not innocent. We're all guilty of something.'

Each and every one of us is haunted by something. It's what makes us human. We all sleep in darkness. It's not the dark you should fear though, it's the light. That's why some things are better left unsaid. Some wounds are too painful to re-open.

Available now in paperback and Kindle, from Amazon.

KEEP IN TOUCH

Sign-up to the newsletter and be the first to receive updates on new and future releases: https://louisemullins2010.wix.com/author

Facebook:
https://www.facebook.com/pages/Scream-Quietly/476430742516844

Twitter:
https://twitter.com/MullinsAuthor

LinkedIn:
https://uk.linkedin.com/in/louisemullinsauthor

Wordpress:
https://louisemullinsauthor.wordpress.com

https://www.goodreads.com/LouiseMullinsAuthor

Printed in Great Britain
by Amazon.co.uk, Ltd.,
Marston Gate.